The Second Time is Easy

Murder is easy—or so Simon Pettifer discovered when he killed the mistress who was threatening to break up his marriage. He even found it surprisingly easy to dispose of her body. As for his wife, all she had to do was keep silent. Polly Gathercole had effectively disappeared.

Of course the police made inquiries, spurred on by Polly's brother, but Simon was ready for them. There was no suspicion in the supermarket where he and Polly worked as manager and till supervisor respectively that their relationship was more than it appeared. Simon agreed that Polly had visited him and his wife socially on the evening of her disappearance, but claimed she had left under her own steam. There was no reason to disbelieve him. Her car was back in her garage; her handbag and its contents unmarked and back in her flat. Even when the police showed interest in the foundations of the home extension the Pettifers were having erected, Simon retained his cool.

It was only later that he lost it, and in circumstances so bizarre that it was understandable if he thought murder the second time was easy. Unfortunately for him, it was not.

by the same author

DEAD HEAT
PRIME TARGET
THE DARKER SIDE OF DEATH
CENSOR
A DOMESTIC AFFAIR
THE SEARCH FOR SARA
ALL PART OF THE SERVICE
RAINBLAST
BACKLASH
CATSPAW
DEATH FUSE
TOUCHDOWN
A DANGEROUS PLACE TO DWELL
DAYLIGHT ROBBERY
DIAL DEATH
MR T
DOUBLE DEAL
MURDER BY THE MILE
THE CLIENT
PHANTOM HOLIDAY
CRIME WAVE
DOUBLE HIT
CONCRETE EVIDENCE
ADVISORY SERVICE
DEADLINE
HUNT TO A KILL
DANGER MONEY
NO RETURN TICKET
NO THROUGH ROAD

MARTIN RUSSELL

The Second Time is Easy

THE CRIME CLUB

COLLINS, 8 GRAFTON STREET, LONDON W1

William Collins Sons & Co. Ltd
London · Glasgow · Sydney · Auckland
Toronto · Johannesburg

To my mother – the sleuth of them all.

First published 1987

British Library Cataloguing in Publication Data

Russell, Martin
The second time is easy.—(Crime Club)
I. Title
823′.914[F] PR6068.U86

ISBN 0 00 232155 6

Photoset in Linotron Baskerville by
Rowland Phototypesetting Ltd
Bury St Edmunds, Suffolk
Printed in Great Britain by
William Collins Sons & Co. Ltd, Glasgow

CHAPTER 1

The first impact was like being leapt upon unexpectedly by a cat. It came out of darkness, out of the oblivion to which she had succumbed, adding a new dimension to the nightmare. Hoping to awake, she lay still.

The second and third impacts were solid enough, but the fearful dream persisted. Already the increasing weight had immobilized her. The pressure on her chest and stomach meant that she could scarcely breathe. Her throat felt inflamed, blocked. Her arms had no power.

It was easier to lie still, to await each succeeding assault as it came. Warmer, too. She had been exposed to the wind: vaguely she remembered that. Now, prostrate on her spine, below the level of the gusts, there was a sensation of helpless languor, not unpleasant. Although somewhere, at a distance, a voice was shouting a warning, she chose not to heed it. The effort needed would have been too great. In a sense, she had been struggling for months. She was worn out.

How many months? Five. She was perfectly clear about that. Twenty-odd weeks: the space of time it took to regress from buoyancy to foundering-point. With the waters closing over her head, she could see it all in perspective; freeze-framed in sharp silhouette, every detail distinct. It was true, then. Back it all surged at the instant of death. Because she was about to die. She saw this just as clearly. The matter was beyond dispute.

When you gave it some thought, it was the old story. One thing leading to another . . .

CHAPTER 2

'We thought,' explained Jo, 'it might be a nice touch to have an interior connecting door. So she wouldn't feel cut off.'

The builder looked pensive. 'Add to your costs.'

'Would it? Much?'

The abstraction of the builder intensified. Detaching himself from the landing banister, by which his cruiserweight bulk had been supported while Jo was outlining her ideas, he wandered off to the rear room and began tapping the outer wall, eyeing its junction with the ceiling. With some diffidence, Jo followed. He was, she estimated, easily the most solidly-constructed male she had come within a mile of since dropping out of the health-and-beauty night class in the village, where the instructor had looked and behaved as if he fed himself upon teak and granite. Simon, by comparison, was a reed. Albeit, she reminded herself, a nicely-proportioned reed. Size wasn't everything.

'What do you think?' she ventured.

Retreating a yard, the builder cocked his chin at the wallpaper. 'You've a cavity wall there, see. Been insulated, right?'

'We had it done when—'

'So you've got yourself a problem before you start.'

'I thought it was just foam.'

'Toxic. You need to be careful, disturbing that stuff.'

'I see. You don't recommend it, then?'

The builder sucked in both cheeks. 'You crackers about this mother of yours?'

'Why do you think we're having an extension put on?'

He grinned back at her. 'Plenty of folk have relatives to live with 'em out of duty, even though they hate their guts. You'd be surprised.'

'Not me. I did social work for a time. I know what people can be like.'

'Social work.' He sounded impressed. 'That must take it out of you. Did you ever find—'

'All I can say is, my mother and I are on good terms, my husband gets on with her and we'd like her to feel one of the family. While keeping,' Jo added sternly, 'her independence.'

'So you want us to bash a hole in this wall and make a door?'

'As long as it doesn't bankrupt us.'

The builder drifted into another trance. 'I'll take a shufty from outside,' he told her eventually, and went off downstairs. His footsteps were light, although the boards shuddered a bit.

Pursuing him to ground-floor level, Jo stationed herself at the living-room window, took a couple of reviving breaths, pocketed both hands in her floral overall and stared out at the garden. She hated this phase. Having the basic idea and developing it was fun. Achieving the end-product would no doubt be rewarding. In between, one had to endure this procedural limbo, this quasi-communication with an intermediary who came packed with a cargo of pre-wrapped practical objections, counter-proposals, qualifications, amendments. The resolution of it all was, of course, merely a matter of time. Like everything else. And the effort was going to be worthwhile. Mother would be grateful. And Simon, thank Heaven, was being remarkably supportive. Many a husband would have given the entire project the thumbs-down.

'Spend whatever's necessary,' he had told her on the note of tolerance he reserved for those occasions when he might justly have been expected to create the maximum fuss. 'If we're having the job done, let's do it properly. Otherwise it's no investment.'

There was a hard-headed side to Simon that was not lost

upon Jo, as she had several times mentioned to her friend Stephanie. With the apparently inexorable rise in property values, it was perhaps not surprising that he should take a relaxed view of what might have seemed horrendous expenditure on accommodation for a mother-in-law. At the same time, he had a soft core. Carol would vouch for that. She could do anything with her father. So perhaps there was genuine philanthropy in his approach to the extension plan, as well as an eye to business. Not that it mattered much. The important thing was that he was cooperating, not throwing up obstacles.

The builder was out of sight. Jo guessed he was investigating the base of the exterior wall, assembling his reservations. In her experience, the multiplicity of caveats with which any contractor was automatically equipped had to be heard to be believed. It was almost as though they were in business to prevent new structures rather than build them. Was it a trick of the trade? Perhaps, like some doctors, they were more intent on sustaining the mystique obscuring their activities than actually doing anything.

She hoped this man was different. He might be. A village acquaintance of theirs had recommended him. He had built the acquaintance a new bathroom, which apparently was still holding together and keeping the rain out after a year: anyone who could accomplish that was surely not a complete idiot. And at least, Jo conceded to herself as she stepped into the garden via the patio door, he seemed easy to talk to. As far as could be judged, he took in what was said and considered it, with an air of private amusement that somehow was not offensive. He had proved, in fact, instantly likeable. Jo had a healthy scepticism of first impressions, but she was allowing herself to be faintly encouraged.

She found him, as expected, exploring with a toe the soil at the base of the outside wall, gazing at the brickwork and humming to himself. Approaching, she coughed humbly.

'What's the verdict?'

Giving the topsoil a rest, the builder withdrew a couple of paces and adopted a posture of assessment. 'Nice bit of mortaring there,' he pronounced finally. 'Shame to interfere with it, really.'

'If you're making an omelette . . .'

'You have to be nice to the hen. How vital is this connecting door of yours?'

'My mother could always come round from her front entrance to ours. She'd have a key to the main house, naturally.'

'Sloppy in damp weather.'

'That's what I was thinking. About how much,' Jo inquired apprehensively, 'would an inside door cost us, do you think?'

'You're looking at an extra six hundred.'

'As much as that?'

'If I could tell you less, Mrs Pettifer, I'd be delighted.'

She studied his face. 'I believe you would be. It's quite a surcharge, isn't it? Needs thinking about. In the meantime, I wonder if we could go into the basic details—room dimensions and so forth? Come back to the house and I'll make some coffee and we'll talk about it.'

'I'm agreeable.'

Inside the kitchen/diner, face to face across steaming beakers, they discussed figures. Mr Hawkins, of Hawkins Constructional, invited her to call him Rod. 'Short for Roderick, not Rodney. Not crazy about either of 'em, to be honest.' The humour glinted again. 'I could do without the Hawkins bit, too, if you must know. Sounds like one of them fancy butlers. So I generally settle for Rod. My missus calls me Beef.' He flexed a bare arm, causing sinew to swell impressively. 'Been a widow long, has she, your mother?'

'My father died three years ago.' Jo said it as briefly as she could. The memory still had power to hurt. 'Since then she's been living on in their rented flat on the outskirts of Guildford, but I think it's been very lonely for her. A lot of her friends have moved away, others have died . . . you know how it is.'

Rod nodded understandingly. 'And of course it don't get any easier, not as you get older.'

'She's very active, for sixty-one. It's just that she feels cut off. So my husband and I discussed it with her and we decided it would be better all round if she came here. We'd be on call, but she could keep to herself whenever she felt inclined.'

'Good thinking' Rod consulted the draft plan he had pencilled on a half-sheet of notepaper. 'Bedsit, kitchenette and bath. Ten by fifteen for the living space . . . That going to be enough?'

'What do you think?' she asked solemnly.

His mouth twitched. 'Depends if your mum wants to organize barn dances four times a week. Personally, I'd go for something like twelve by twenty, and maybe cut down on the other measurements so as to pack it all into the same external footage. Does she run a car?'

'No. She's like me, useless in traffic.'

'No garaging needed, then. All she wants is the basics. Single storey, pitched roof, stocks and tiles in harmony with existing. Now let's take a look . . .'

Rod's tongue-tip protruded as he hunched himself over the sketch plan and began scrawling marginal comments and suggestions. Thankful to concede the initiative, Jo sipped dreamily at her coffee and tried to visualize the everyday routine once her mother was alongside them. Any problems, she hoped, would be outweighed by the benefits. Carol would enjoy having her Nan close at hand. As for Simon, he was seldom at home long enough to represent a possible threat to serenity. Not that such a development was likely, in Jo's opinion. Simon had always taken his mother-in-law in his faintly patronizing stride, addressed her with kindness, exhibited tolerance of her quirks. If Jo had a complaint, it was that his attitude seemed to incorporate an air of indulgent superiority, giving the impression that he regarded his widowed relative as more simple-minded than was the case; although Jo was forced to admit that her mother appeared unaware of any condescension in his manner. Probably she, Jo, imagined a great deal. It was just Simon's way. Himself quick-brained, alert to opportunities, he was perhaps prone to underrate the opposition in commercial terms, and this could reflect itself in his personal relationships. In her quiet way, Jo studied him acutely and kept score. His early rise to supermarket branch manager was, she felt, well merited, but he would have to watch his step.

'What you've got, then,' announced Rod, emerging from his calculations, 'is three rooms plus entrance lobby, brick on concrete, tiling to roof, all integral to main structure: exact dimensions to be decided, finishings subject to choice, flagged pathway between entrances . . . *no* internal connecting door.' He twisted an eyebrow in Jo's direction. 'Right? Or am I twisting your arm?'

She smiled back at him. 'Sounds fine. When can you let us have an estimate?'

Draining his beaker, Rod smacked it down, rose with a gasp. 'I'll get back and work on it. Should be able to give you some idea inside a couple of days. Then you can chat it over with your old man, see what he thinks about it.' He stood looking down at her. 'Nice to do business with you, Mrs Pettifer. Hope to be seeing you again.'

'Please call me Jo.' It emerged awkwardly, making her, she judged irritably, sound stuffy. She tried again. 'Short for Joanna, not Josephine. In case you were wondering.'

'Nice names, both of 'em. I've a girlfriend called Jo-Anne. Annie, I call her. Silly, isn't it? Just sounds right, for her.'

Jo regarded him warily. 'I must have misheard. I thought I understood you to say you were married . . . ?'

'That's right. You've got it.'

'So Annie is an *ex*-girlfriend?'

Rod shook a cheerful head. 'Very much on the current register. Won't leave us alone, you see. Reckons I'm the choicest hunk of flesh since the fatted calf. She's a fancy bit of goods herself, so it's okay by me.'

Jo did her best to keep her mouth from falling open. 'Doesn't your wife have anything to say about it?'

'Now and then,' he admitted. 'Generally speaking, though, she lets us do what I like. Long as I come up with the necessary—I'm talking about material comforts—I'm allowed to express myself when I'm safely out of her sight. She doesn't really want to know.'

'Can you be sure of that?'

He thought about it, gravely. 'Can't be certain of anything, can we? Any of us. All I do know is, if Mo—that's my missus—ever wanted a bit on the side herself, she'd be welcome . . . only she always says she don't. Well, that's up to her, isn't it? I've given her the green light. Can't do more.'

'I'm sure that's a comfort to her.' Jo contrived to keep her broadminded expression balanced on her face, although it was starting to wobble precariously. Reclaiming the empty beakers, she took them to the sink and ran hot water over them. When she turned, Rod was regarding her with a friendly half-smile that made her at once mollified and uneasy. 'You're a child of the times,' she said severely. 'You want everything immediately, on credit.'

'You're right, Jo,' he said earnestly. 'You've struck it in one.'

At a loss how to react, she shook her head in the manner of a school headteacher faced by a perplexing drop in the standard of a star pupil's work. 'As long as you don't come a cropper. You could, you know. The worm might turn. It happens.'

'If Mo was thinking of turning,' the builder said reflectively, 'she'd of done it by now. She's had cause enough.'

'Hmp. Annie's not the first, then?'

'Nor likely to be the last, neither.' Rod spoke with the

reasoned confidence of a man alive to his destiny. There was, Jo found to her puzzlement, nothing boastful or objectionable in his manner; he was simply enlightening her as to the state of affairs, in response to her initial query. He was neither diffident about it, nor assertive. As though sensing that the dialogue had gone far enough, he added, 'Anyway, you don't want to hear about my love-life. What you're interested in is how much this little lot—' he gestured at the outer wall—'is going to set you back, right? I'll have that estimate on your doormat by first post Thursday morning, latest. Can't say fairer, can I?'

'Thursday would be great.' Opening the kitchen door, she placed the palm of tolerance against his massive elbow to steer him through to the hall. To her faint alarm he stayed where he was, thirteen stone of meat and muscle between door and frame, looking down at her with calm, appraising eyes.

'See you then, Jo. Not too long, I hope.'

She tried to laugh it off. 'That rather depends on the estimate.'

'Better pitch it low, then, hadn't I?'

'If you want the job. There are other contractors, you know.'

'And a right bunch of piranhas they are, too,' he said without resentment. After another second or two of silent scrutiny, he turned and clumped away down the hall. 'You'll like my work,' he told her from the front door, 'and I won't rook you for it. Not you, Jo. That's a promise.' He flashed her an amiable row of teeth. 'So long.'

The door shut behind him. Moments later the van door slammed, the motor snorted, gravel scattered as he drove off. Jo stood listening to the vehicle's dwindling howl as it gathered pace along the lane. Presently she returned slowly to the kitchen sink where hot water was still wasting itself down the pipe. Mechanically she turned it off, staring to her left through the window at the semi-wild, wooded garden that had appealed so strongly to her and Simon when they first chanced upon the property. Normally, the sight of it had an instantly soothing effect. This time it continued to be slightly more difficult than usual to take regular breaths. Her knees felt shaky.

CHAPTER 3

'Jo's quite fond of her mother.' Arranging himself over the length of the white leather-wrapped couch, Simon rotated the martini glass in his fingers as a luxurious preliminary to placing it to his lips. 'That's why she's dead set on this notion of an annexe. I don't honestly have much choice.'

His mistress, Polly Gathercole, glided across the woolly carpet with her own wineglass to establish herself against the back end of the couch, allowing one plump knee to escape the embrace of her bright yellow robe while keeping Simon under the level, unblinking surveillance that operated so effectively on behalf of the lip-glossed visions in the TV soaps to which Polly was shamelessly addicted. After an interval she said huskily, 'Why not?'

'Why don't I have a choice? You've got to be joking.'

'I never joke before six.' Polly's large brown eyes smouldered. She knew they were smouldering, because she had practised the procedure in the mirror for some weeks and prided herself that she had now honed it to perfection. 'You've always said the house is too big for you, as it is. Why add to it?'

'It's not *that* much too big. We've a spare bedroom, that's all. Carol has the attic, so that's not available. If Jo's mother tacks herself on to us, she'll need separate facilities of her own.'

'I'd have thought she could live in.'

'Poll, for God's sake. I'd go barmy in a fortnight.'

'I thought you didn't mind her that much.'

'She sends me up the wall. She's so bloody *humble*. Uriah Heep's not in it. If it was genuine I wouldn't mind, but it's not. Basically, she thinks she knows best. For everyone.'

'And you don't, of course.' Polly gave him a look of affectionate realism.

'At least I make no bones about it.' She liked that about him: he could take a dig or two, at any rate from her. She enjoyed the sensation of power that it gave her, though she was careful never to go too far. He took an abrupt gulp of his martini. 'Doris does it all under cover. Pretends to be submissive, when all the time she's . . . I don't know. Maybe I'm being unfair. But I think she could cause a bit of harm.'

'Who to?'

'Carol, for one. Doris has funny ideas about kids.'

'*You* think they're funny.'

'No, I'm serious. She's old-fashioned in her outlook. Doesn't realize the world's moved on. If she gets the chance to influence Carol in the wrong way . . .'

'Aha.'

Simon glanced up. 'What do you mean, "Aha"?'

'You're starting to sound a bit possessive, Simon my sweet.'

'Rubbish. I want Carol to have someone she can . . . look up to. Just as long as she's not alienated from those who really have her interests at heart.'

'Like her dad, for instance?'

'I'm the only father she's got,' he said stiffly.

'And I'm sure Carol appreciates it.' Polly studied him curiously. 'What exactly are you afraid Jo's mother might do to her?'

Simon shrugged. 'You know how kids can be swayed. At nine years old, Carol's ripe for guidance. I want it to be the right sort.'

'You mean, you want to be the one to give it to her?'

'If you like.'

'Where does this leave me?'

He met her gaze. 'I don't see that it leaves you anywhere. Not planning a domestic upheaval, are we?'

'Aren't we?'

He said nothing. Polly sat tapping her prominent front teeth gently with the rim of the wineglass. 'What you're saying,' she suggested after another prolonged pause, 'seems to amount to a first-class reason for *not* having Jo's mother to live near you. Why don't you plant your foot down?'

'Because, my love, my chief aim at the moment is to stay out of trouble with Jo.'

'I get it.'

'Besides, there could be advantages to the scheme. If Jo has her mother living alongside, she won't get lonesome during the day—correct? Consequently there'd be less restraint on my movements. Correct, again?'

'Does she get lonesome?'

'Jo? I've never asked her.'

'Maybe you should.'

'Why?'

Sitting back, Polly surveyed him. 'Most women quite like to have a little interest shown in these matters.'

Simon looked up again sharply. 'Do I detect an edge?'

'Depends how sensitive a touch you've got.'

Draping an arm over the back of the couch, Simon deposited his glass on an onyx-topped table just within reach, before rising to his feet with a frown. 'Something you're trying to tell me, Poll?'

She glanced up at him with a smile. 'A girl has her feelings.'

'You're finding the situation irksome. That it?'

'How long have we known each other, Simon?'

He made swift calculations. 'You joined the firm in August last year. A month or so later—'

'You first took me out on September the sixth.'

'You made a note of it?'

'Didn't have to. It's the kind of date I happen to remember. Obviously it didn't make the same impression on you. Okay—I'm not complaining. Men are different. It just helps to make my point, that's all.'

'What precisely is your point?'

'I think you know.'

Striding restively to the curtains, Simon checked the security of the join between them, stood in an irresolute stance for a moment, came back, dropped boyishly to a crouch beside her.

'I do know, Poll,' he told her, taking a handful of her fingers. 'You feel shut out. You're not totally a part of my life. You feel badly about Jo. I understand all that.'

Extracting her fingers, she turned her face away. 'You're a sweet, understanding guy.'

From the corner of an eye she saw uncertainty filter into his expression. He said, 'I try to be.'

'When it suits you.'

'That's unfair. Right from the start of our relationship—'

'Oh yes, yes. Everything laid on the line. No question of leaving your wife, much too fond of your daughter, couldn't stand losing custody, anyway too much consideration for poor Jo, not to mention the financial angle . . . Nobody can say you didn't set it out.'

'And having looked at the display,' he said quietly, 'you approved it. If you recall.'

'Accommodating, that's me.'

'But you're now having second thoughts?'

'Thoughts? What does thought have to do with it?'

Back on his heels, Simon regarded her intently. From the adjoining flat, the faint whump-whump of a stereo release pulsed into the room, an alien heartbeat disturbing the cardiograph. The air was getting baked. Even in mid-May, Polly liked her comforts. The central heating was full on. Although she was not looking at him, she knew that there were sweat patches on his shirt. They were not, she hoped, entirely due to the room temperature.

She had not planned a confrontation, but now that it had occurred she was rather enjoying it. All the frustration and resentment of the past few months was welling to the surface. She wanted to hit out.

The trouble was, Simon was adroit at riding punches. Uncoiling himself, he took the wineglass gently from her grasp and placed it next to the other on the onyx table. A four-inch strip of the couch by Polly was available: he took occupation. His hands went to work. One on the left shoulder, the other in the region of the waistline. At his touch, she wriggled.

'Knock it off, Simon.'

'Just relax. We can't talk while you're strung up like a concert grand.'

'There's nothing to talk about.'

'Then don't say a word. Ease those muscles. Just let yourself—'

Polly's wriggle became a convulsive movement, culminating in her withdrawal and re-grouping at the far end of the room, where she stood making critical adjustments to the hang of her robe. 'Right this minute,' she informed him, retying the cord and inspecting it for distortion, 'I don't happen to feel in an easy or relaxed frame of mind. So it's a bit of a waste of time, isn't it? If you've finished your drink, you might as well be on your way. You don't want to keep your wife hanging about. She might start to wonder what's holding you up.'

'Look, do we have to—'

'And that's just one of the things you've got to avoid, isn't it? At all costs.'

'Poll, you're being stupid.'

'Oh, sorry. I hadn't realized that. I was under the delusion I was helping you maintain your undefeated record—nine months not caught out. Now that you mention it, I do see that I'm being utterly illogical and unreasonable and lacking in brainpower. Try to overlook it. Some of us don't measure up to the giant intellects we make contact with, though we do our puny best. Can you forgive me?'

Simon went across to a corner chair to collect his jacket. 'I think,' he said, punching an arm through a sleeve, 'I'd better be leaving.'

'You seem to have got the message.'

'You're in a funny mood.'

'I'm glad you find it amusing.'

'I don't. I can't imagine what's got into you, but I'm damned if I intend to stop around to find out. I've better things to do with my time.'

'Like placating a suspicious wife?' Although inwardly dismayed, Polly had reached the stage of verbal recklessness.

'Jo's not suspicious.'

'Oh, great. Haven't you done well? No slip-ups, no messy little blots on the account-sheet. All tidy and pigeonholed. Nothing for anybody to complain of.'

He headed for the door. 'I'll see you tomorrow.'

'Don't count on it.'

Simon paused. 'You're on duty from eight-thirty, in case you'd forgotten. Unless you're thinking of handing in your notice . . .'

'I'm seriously considering it.'

'Don't be childish. Sleep on it.'

'I'll sleep,' she assured him, marching across to pummel the cushions on which he had sprawled. 'I hope the same goes for you.'

CHAPTER 4

The traffic roar from the Guildford road was even-handed in its generosity—no home within half a mile was left to feel neglected—but Doris Kersh didn't mind that. 'Does me good, hearing the motors,' she was fond of remarking. 'Bit of life, isn't it? Lets you know things are going on.'

In her younger days, Doris had doted on trams. During the London Blitz, their distant groanings had come unfailingly to the aid of her and her family, night after night. 'After an air raid,' she would tell anybody who would listen, 'you'd hear them trams start up again, scraping and moaning over the lines, and you'd know there was people still alive and kicking—things was getting back to normal.' The usual reaction from her listeners was a tolerant smile. Most of them, as Jo had tried to explain to her, had not been around during the Blitz. It made no difference. Regardless of the response, or lack of one, Jo's mother still enjoyed talking about the War.

Luckily for her, Ethel Fairchild in Flat 16 on the floor below had likewise been born an East Ender and was seldom averse to an orgy of reminiscence. She was one of the people whom Doris knew she would miss, if and when she moved out of Rowan Court. Ethel was the closest thing she had to a bosom chum, even if they didn't always see eye to eye. She, in return, would miss Doris. Both of them were widows, and they had got used to one another.

'You might find it a bit deadly,' Ethel sniffed, ramming teabags into a pot. 'Miles from anywhere. Wouldn't do for me.'

'You've not got family there,' Doris pointed out complacently, eyeing the plateful of assorted biscuits that Ethel had shoved under her chin. 'It'll be quiet, I dare say. Shan't have time to twiddle me thumbs, though. Be run off me feet, more like. Jo'll be wanting some help with the housework.'

'That why she's having you to live?'

'If you want my opinion, she's a bit lonesome herself.' Selecting a custard cream, Doris attacked it with her front teeth. 'Keen to have her mum to fall back on. What with Carol being at school, Simon out at that supermarket all day long . . .'

Ethel sniffed again. 'What's the name of the village, did you say?'

'Melking. Back of the Downs, six miles from Southweald.'

'Sounds like a graveyard. You'll go potty.'

'Lots to do in Southweald,' said Doris, munching comfortably. 'Shops and the seafront and everything. A friend of Jo's in the village, she takes her in by car sometimes. I could go along. Or Simon might take us, and I could get the bus back.'

'How does he fancy having you around?'

'Haven't asked him.'

'You might fight.'

'We've not, up till now. We get on. Anyhow, don't forget, Eth, I shan't be living in the same house as them. They're having an extension built on.'

Ethel flooded the teabags with scalding water. 'A granny flat,' she snorted.

'A linked annexe,' Doris corrected her graciously. 'I can be entirely self-contained, if I want to be. Shut meself right off. Jo's got it all planned.'

'Don't seem much point moving there, if you're going to hide yourself away.'

'Who said anything about hiding? What I meant, it's an escape, like, if things start getting on top of us. No reason why they should. Jo's easygoing. As for Carol, I can do anything I like with her. She's a good little kid.'

'We'll be sorry to lose you from here,' Ethel said grudgingly, replenishing the teacups. 'When is it you're going?'

'Oh, not for a while. The fl—the annexe isn't even built yet. Jo phoned yesterday to say she'd spoken to the builder and he's going to give them an estimate. Then they have to get permission and it all takes time. I'll still be here in the autumn, I reckon.'

The telephone rasped as Doris, two days later, was settling down to watch the only televised sitcom of the entire week that did not rely for laughs exclusively upon human bodily functions and infidelity. The caller was Simon. A little put out, Doris nevertheless poured warmth into her voice. 'Hullo, Simon dear. Any trouble? Jo not well?'

'She's fine. She and her friend Stephanie have gone to the cinema in Southweald, so she asked me to give you a buzz. It's just to let you know that we've had a draft estimate from the builder which seems reasonable—by current yardsticks, that is. Nothing too outrageous.'

'Oh. That's good, isn't it?'

'So we've asked him for detailed plans and so forth. Of course, there'll be some delay before the job can start. Planning permission . . . that's sure to hold things up.'

'Can't hurry them, can you?' Doris knew nothing of the procrastination of local authorities, but felt it diplomatic to show an intelligent interest. 'Be worth it, though, in the end. It's ever so good of you, Simon, to be going to all this bother. I don't want to be a nuisance . . .'

A half-laugh rippled the wire. 'We're feathering our own nest, Doris, besides providing one for you. We hope it'll be a sound investment all round.'

'I hope so, too,' said Doris, a little dashed. She paused. 'Quite sure you won't mind having me live so close? I wouldn't want to cramp your—'

'Don't be daft. We want to get you nicely settled. Carol's looking forward to your arrival.'

'Bless her. How is she?'

'Sends her love. She's at ballet class this evening, in the village.'

'You won't let her walk back, Simon, by herself?'

'Stop panicking. I'm off right now to pick her up. Regarding the annexe, we'll keep you posted on developments. Hard to give you a likely moving-in date, at this stage. Once the actual building starts, it shouldn't take long. What eats up the time is all the preliminary—'

'Don't you worry, dear. I'm not the impatient sort, as

you know. Soon as I get the word, I'll be glad to come trotting along: up until then, I'm quite all right where I am. You're all keeping well, then?'

'Pretty fair. Overwork is my main complaint. Too many people breathing down my neck, wanting to cash in on the consumer boom.'

'I suppose you can't blame them. Never mind, dear. Won't be long now before you're head of the chain. Then you can boss 'em all around, can't you? Get things done your way.'

'If I last that long. 'Bye for now, Doris. We'll be in touch.'

CHAPTER 5

'Any news of the loan?'

'Nope.' Simon flipped the three opened buff envelopes aside to launch an assault on his grilled sausage. 'But don't worry about it. The bank virtually guaranteed the money.'

'Banks,' said Jo pessimistically, 'have been known to change their minds.'

'Even if they did, which is unlikely, there are other sources.' He spoke patiently, too patiently, on a faintly audible intake of breath, as though to a willing but cloth-headed pupil.

Jo waited a few moments. 'What do you think of Rod's final plans?'

'Competent.'

'It's not a rival to the Taj Mahal we're after,' she pointed out. 'As long as it tones in with the rest of the house and doesn't leak. I'm still wondering about a connecting door. What's your opinion?'

'Have one. If you think your mother would like it.'

'It'll cost us. And I'm not sure that she would.'

Eliminating a mouthful of sausage, Simon sat back and

pondered. 'You mean, she might see it as an invasion of privacy?'

'Or you might.'

He stared out at the garden. 'If we're having Doris to live here,' he observed presently, 'I can't see much sense in doing it by halves—inviting her along with one hand, holding her off with the other. Either she's with us or she's not. Personally, I'm in favour of her having ready access, if that's what she wants. I'm sure she wouldn't abuse the privilege.'

It sounded condescending, thought Jo, but probably Simon hadn't meant it that way. He really was being very good-hearted about the whole thing: she must bear that in mind. It helped to make up for other deficiencies in Simon's manner that she hadn't been able to help noticing of late. 'More toast?' she inquired.

Instead of a reply she got another question. 'You think the two of you will get along?'

'Mother and I? Good heavens, yes. We've hardly ever exchanged a cross word.'

'Cheek by jowl, things could be different.'

'They won't be,' Jo said with confidence. 'We understand one another too well.'

'Then what's the problem?' Rising, Simon grabbed the envelopes and stowed them inside his briefcase. 'Ask Rod to put in a connecting door and try to keep the price under a thousand. The more I think about it, the more it strikes me it'll be money well spent.'

'All right. Thanks. I'll speak to him about it today.'

'Is he coming along?'

'He said he'd drop by to get the plans back. They have to be copied for submission to the council.'

Simon brushed her nose with a featherlight kiss in passing. 'Tell him to push things through as fast as he can. We don't want it dragging on for a year. Talking of delay, I might be home a bit late this evening.'

'How late?'

'Can't say. We've some stock discrepancies to check on. I'll try to make it before nine.'

'The sooner Mother gets here,' Jo said on what was intended to be a humorous note, 'the sooner I'll stop being an abandoned wife, six evenings of the week.'

'Not that bad, surely? I was home by seven last night.'

'The effort must have nearly killed you.'

Simon paused at the foot of the stairs. ''Bye, darling,' he called up them. Overhead, a door opened.

'Bye-bye, Daddy.' Carol charged down to be hugged. 'Will you be home in time for *Kidnapped*?' she demanded.

'Doubt it. You'll have to tell me how it ends.'

'Don't you *know*?'

'I'm not quite up with my classics. Have a nice day, sweetheart. Work hard.'

Jo accompanied him out to the porch. 'Looks like being a scorcher,' she remarked as he ducked into his Renault automatic waiting on the gravel. 'If you get half-blinded by figurework, try for a lunch-time stroll along the promenade. Do you good. Otherwise you'll crack up. We don't want you making yourself ill. How's Polly? Is she back yet?'

His head re-emerged. 'What?'

'Polly—your till supervisor or whatever she is. Did she get over her laryngitis?'

'Back next Monday, it's rumoured.' Simon didn't sound interested. She wondered, momentarily, whether he was good with his staff. To be true manager material you had to involve yourself, surely, with those under you? Simon often gave the impression that he simply didn't care. At times, he was almost too dismissive: it was like an elaborate pose. Especially in recent weeks. To hear him talk, you'd think the store was manned by a bunch of humanoids, engineered in company workshops. The only reason Jo knew of Polly's laryngitis was that she had telephoned Simon in his office one day and Polly had chanced to answer, and had mentioned the affliction, hoarsely and with difficulty.

The following day, Jo had inquired after her and Simon had said she was taking a week or two off. His manner was completely indifferent. He might have been talking about one of his own joints of beef. In fact, Jo thought, had he been doing so, his voice would doubtless have betrayed more concern. Men were a puzzlement.

'Drive carefully,' she mouthed, giving the rear of the Renault a final wave as it took off down the drive.

Returning into the house, Jo paused suddenly on her way to the kitchen.

A thought that she hadn't known was lying submerged had bobbed unexpectedly to the surface, knocking the breath out of her. She had no wish to give it the slightest attention. For some reason, however, it refused to sink back, stay out of sight and hearing. To help smother it, she hurried on through to the kitchen sink and did her best impression of the little housewife, producing a great deal of noise and steam. It failed to achieve much.

'Your main problem,' advised Rod Hawkins, stepping with massive care over a struggling conifer situated midway between the designated site and the house, 'is liable to be Drainage. Not mains-connected, are you?'

'No, but we've never had any trouble. There's a soak-away.' Jo pointed. 'Over there somewhere, at the foot of the slope.'

The builder shaded his eyes. 'Septic tank?'

'I've no idea,' she said blankly. 'My husband could tell you.'

'Only, if that's the case, you wouldn't want storm water adding itself to the load. We might be able to get round that.' Rod aimed himself in the direction Jo had indicated. 'Let's go take a look.'

'While you're doing that, I'll make some coffee.'

He looked down at her benevolently. 'If it's all the same to you, I'd sooner you came along, showed us where you mean. I wouldn't want to trample your plants.'

'You won't find many down there,' shè told him. 'It's been left to grow wild. Anyway, we trust you.'

Rod tutted, shook his head. 'Never trust anybody. That's the only way to live. I could be the clumsiest bloody mortal this side of the English Channel, couldn't I? You don't know.'

'This garden was designed for a regiment of tanks. How do you like your coffee? I've got fresh cream, or you can—'

He took her arm. 'Never you mind about instant granules or suchlike, for the minute. Show us this soakaway of yours. Lovely morning. Make a nice little saunter for you, bottom of the garden and back.'

'I really ought to be—'

'Now, Jo. A girl like you shouldn't be letting herself get too domesticated. You're not the type.'

'Oh? What type am I?'

Wrong retort. Its emergence had been involuntary, powered by the high-octane alarm that had flooded her as his fingers closed with gentle relentlessness on the flesh above her elbow. Beneath her reluctant feet, the ground squelched a little as they headed side by side for the boundary fence. The day before, it had rained steadily for five hours, climaxing a prolonged wet period that had driven the population to despair of the arrival of summer. Now, in contrast, the weather looked set fair. Beyond the partly-wooded fields on the far side of the fence, the Downs reared startlingly into the blue, like miniature Alpine foothills. Chalk paths meandered to the top, but nobody was on them. It was only the weekend trippers who attempted the climb. The locals never bothered.

As Simon was fond of remarking, it was as good as having your own mountain range in your backyard. Ideal, Jo had often thought wistfully, for dogs. She wished they could have a pet. But Simon didn't care for animals, and Carol was in any case allergic to canine coats. Perhaps later . . .

'Type?' Picking his way lazily across hummocks, Rod squinted into the sun. 'Adventurous, I'd say. Game for a crack at most things. Not inclined to be tied down.'

She had contrived to disengage her arm. But she was keeping pace with him, half-mesmerized into going along with what seemed to be little more than a whim on his part, a flippant diversion loosely disguised as duty. If she turned back now, it would look offensive. The alternative was to sound jocular. 'Should I be flattered?'

'That's for you to decide.' Rod half-turned to glance back at the house. 'Nice, south-facing aspect you've got. Why don't I build you a solarium over them sliding doors? Do a spot of nude sunbathing inside there, you could.'

'Let's get the extension done first, shall we?'

'Keep it in mind, though.'

'You must think we're made of money.'

'Needn't cost you a bomb. For you, Jo, I'd do a real package job.'

'Why would you?'

'Why? Because I'm a sucker for a smile.' A brief explosion of mirth rocked him in his tracks. 'How's that for cards on the table? You've got to me, Jo—you know that? I'm a sick man. Lovesick. All your fault.'

'Sorry. I never intended to spread the virus.'

He pulled a face. 'Some bugs do you less damage than others. So they tell me. Secluded here, aren't you? No neighbours.'

'Actually,' explained Jo, keeping at a yard's distance from him, 'they're closer than you might think. Just the other side of those trees is Barker's Farm—we're always getting the noise of their tractors. Over there is Downsview Cottage. It's occupied by old Mrs Turner, whose twin sons—'

'Okay, I didn't ask for a breakdown of the neighbourhood. This the spot you were meaning?'

'I believe so,' Jo said thankfully. 'You can see the manhole covers . . . there should be three of them. I expect you've come across a similar arrangement before.'

Rod made no comment. Wading through damp grass to the nearest manhole, he stooped, grasped the ring of the metal cover, yanked it upwards. Having gazed down for a moment, he let the cover fall back with a clang and said, 'Hmm.'

'Problems?' Jo inquired anxiously.

Retracing his steps, he rested his spine against a nearby silver birch and took a pack of cigarettes from his hip pocket. He held it out. At the shake of her head he stowed the pack again, untouched, pocketed the other hand, stood watching her. Convinced that he had discovered some insurmountable obstacle to the development, she moved closer.

'Don't tell me. There's not enough capacity, you're going to have to sink another outlet, it'll take six months, cost an extra five thousand?'

He waited a moment. 'What would you do if I said you was right?'

'Go away and shoot myself.'

His sudden grin made an appearance. 'Save your ammo. The tank's fine. No expansion needed.'

Jo sagged and puffed. 'From the look on your face, I thought you were about to—'

'Weight off your mind, huh?'

'You can say that again.'

'So what do I get for it?'

'Coffee and biscuits. I might even chuck in a doughnut. You like doughnuts?'

He made a body movement. 'Tell you what I do have an appetite for, Jo . . .'

'Now don't be silly. You've a wife and a girlfriend. You don't want to exceed your quota.'

'Who's counting?'

'You should be. It's not fair on . . . either of them. You needn't think I approve. I'm all against it.'

'It's not your approval I'm after,' he said mildly.

'I think we'd better go back to the house.' Jo couldn't quite believe that this was happening. Although she was responding with worldly detachment, secretly she was terrified. Up to now, Rod had kept it all low-key: she sensed, however, that if provoked he could explode quite easily and do a considerable amount of damage. He was so immense. 'Let's talk business,' she coaxed him, turning away in the hope that he would trail her in the direction of sanity. 'There are one or two features of your plan I'd like explained, and I'd also appreciate a breakdown of the various . . .'

Physical restraint came as a nasty shock. This time it was both arms. She struggled, panting from fright as well as exertion. 'What are you doing? Leave go of me.'

'I've a better idea, Jo-Jo. Try relaxing. I'm not one of these guys that enjoy resistance. That's not my style. Not yours, either, I can tell that. We're two of a kind, I reckon. So why not make it easy for both of us?'

'You want me to scream?' The dialogue, she thought dizzily, came straight from the pages of pulp fiction; on the other hand, maybe the hack authors had had it right all the time. When it came to the crunch, alternative phraseology of greater elegance was in short supply. 'Don't think I wouldn't. I'm perfectly capable of—'

The sentence ended in a gasp as his arms tightened about her waist. His strength was enormous. With sickening clarity, she recognized the size of her underestimation: Simon at his wildest moments was a five-year-old by comparison. She could no longer talk. Much of the breath had been squeezed from her lungs. Her legs kicked out feebly, achieving no contact. Rod handled her as he might have dealt with half a sack of cement, at arm's length, with economy of movement. A vision of Carol's face flashed across her mind. Anger joined forces suddenly with the terror. Rationalize, she instructed herself. No need to become just another statistic. Counter-attack.

She went limp. Instantly his grip slackened. It gave her back the breath she needed.

'More comfortable . . . back at the house.'

'Okay,' he said amiably.

Preceding him across the rough ground, she thrashed her mind into feats of gymnastics she had never dreamt it could produce. Run? At school she had been a sprinter. Since Carol's birth, however, she had scarcely broken into a trot: Rod was a working builder, fit and active, with legs like scaffolding poles. The house interior? More promising. She alone knew of locks that turned, doors that bolted. Once she was inside . . .

But even if she could work something, little would be gained but time. Sooner or later he would smash the door down.

Reverse the procedure. Entice him into a bedroom, withdraw swiftly while he was off guard, turn the key from outside . . .

Every key in the house was on the inside. There wouldn't be time to make the switch.

The telephone. Three whirls of the dial and a patrol car could be along in minutes. All she needed was a few seconds. He'd allow her that, of course. He'd stand aside in his gentlemanly fashion, offer her the receiver. 'Want to make a call? You just go right ahead, Jo-Jo, while I turn down the bed-cover . . .'

She glanced across a shoulder. 'We can use the attic. Carol's bed is quite roomy.'

'What's wrong with yours?'

'My husband comes back sometimes during the day. If he does, he might have occasion to go into our bedroom.'

'Why does he come back?'

'To consult his stock-sheets. They're stored on computer at Granger's, but sometimes it goes on the blink. So he finds it useful to keep a separate record here.' The glibness of the string of lies was a revelation to herself. 'Not much risk, though. If we stay quiet while he's around, he'll assume I'm out shopping.'

Jo tripped over a tussock. Recovering, she found that her brain had suffered a white-out; the supply of falsehoods had been turned off at the main. She continued to walk mechanically, aware of his closeness at her heels, certain that she could feel his breath, or was it the hot sun on her neck? Most of the garden was now being doused in late spring geniality: a thrush was carolling from the forsythia bush at the edge of the terrace.

She jumped as a hand touched her shoulder. 'Not the house. Keep walking.'

'What?'

'Round to the front. Climb in the van.'

'Look. I've said there's no need to worry. As long as we stay in Carol's room, out of sight . . .'

'We'll be out of sight in the wagon. Away from here.'

She managed a shrug. 'Seems pointless to me. Besides, I can't be away long. Carol's due home for lunch at twelve.'

'She has lunch at school.'

'No, she doesn't.' Wildly improvising, Jo stumbled on. 'She used to, but we found they were doing her no good. She's got a delicate stomach. So she comes back and I cook her something. If she finds I'm not here, she'll probably raise the alarm.'

Behind her, there was an extended silence. Her steps slowed, began to drag, finally halted of their own accord. She turned hesitantly to face him. His expression as he gazed down at her was that of a faintly puzzled man. His head tilted to the left.

'You trying to tell us something, Jo-Jo?'

'Only that we have to be practical. I do have family responsibilities. I can't just—'

'Okay, love. I get the message.'

His tone was regretful, and yet humorous. 'Nearly dropped a clanger there, didn't I? Thought I had you nicely on the boil. What happened to the old magic? I must be losing my touch.'

Jo could think of nothing to say.

'I'm a good builder, Jo-Jo, but I had you wrongly sized up and no mistake. I thought you . . . Forget it. Sorry if I startled you.'

'Don't worry about it,' she said faintly.

'I won't, love, if you won't.'

'I'm afraid I must have misled you . . .'

'I wouldn't say that. Fooled myself, didn't I? Casanova Hawkins flops again. Ah well, you can't win 'em all.' He gave her his friendliest smile. 'What do you say we go back inside, take a dekko at the plans, like you said? And you can make us that coffee.'

'Rod, I really am sorry.'

'Me too. Had it all mapped out, I did. Been looking forward to it all the week.'

Jo gave a sudden helpless shriek of laughter. The force of it sent her staggering across the turf. 'I've never come across anyone like you. How can you just stand there, looking so cheery about it? You're meant to be embarrassed.'

'Why should I be, if you're not?'

'But I am! I'm in knots.'

She hooted again. Rod chimed in obligingly, and together they reeled about the lawn. 'I'm not expecting anyone home,' she spluttered, clinging to his wrist. 'I'm on my own here until four.'

'I know.'

'They were all big fat lies.'

'I *know*.'

'So what are we going to do about it?'

They stood looking at one another. Rod gave a gentle shake of the head. 'I don't know, but we've five hours or so to do it in, by my estimation.'

She said breathlessly, 'Do you have another job to go to?'

'To tell you the honest truth, Mrs Pettifer, trade's a bit on the slack side, just now. My time is yours.'

CHAPTER 6

Doubling herself into her four-year-old Ford Fiesta, Polly Gathercole let in the clutch a shade violently and took off in a smelly singeing of rubber.

Until the very last moment, she had been afraid of changing her mind.

Taking the main London road out of Southweald, she turned off at the third set of traffic lights and climbed a sharp gradient to the top of the Downs. From there she descended at a reckless pace to the lesser highway which skirted the northern foot of the hills. Back on level ground, she followed the signs pointing to Melking, reducing speed to give herself time to think.

A hazardous indulgence. Second thoughts had a habit, she knew, of stifling enterprise. Mingled with Polly's Irish blood, however, was a dash of dourest Scottish which throughout her life had intervened at her wilder moments to counsel caution. And with what result?

With the result, she reminded herself despondently, that at the ripe age of thirty-one she remained marooned in the situation from which she had started out: available but unattached. Always, at the crucial point, she had drawn back. Something better would happen along. The fear of premature commitment had protected her at every turn, and finally had become a cage of steel. Past thirty and thickening at the waist, Polly was starting in desperation to rattle the cage door, doing her best to summon the resolve for a decisive shoulder-heave.

Nobody's looks lasted for ever. True, Simon liked what

he called a cuddlesome build; as yet, Polly felt moderately sure, he had not begun to tire of her somewhat overblown endowments. She could count on breathing space before he commenced to carp, to find fault where previously he had admired. Before that happened, she wanted to be certain of him.

MELKING: 2 miles.

The sign at the intersection stirred the butterflies dozing inside her stomach, set them fluttering in nauseating swarms. Clenching her teeth, she swung the car in the direction indicated and forced herself to accelerate.

The house was larger than Polly had expected. From the way Simon had spoken, she had envisaged a poky cottage conversion crammed into the end of a lane. The double-fronted, stone-and-tile edifice that confronted her as she steered the Fiesta between a couple of ruts and through the gateway leading into the drive was a major surprise. What did they want with a granny annexe? From the look of it, the existing structure had room for the four of them and to spare.

Exasperation with Simon's profligacy reassembled in Polly's chest. The squandering of money for its own sake was something she had always despised. It was one of the traits she planned to relieve him of, once she had made sure of him.

A builder's van was parked at the head of the drive. R. G. HAWKINS, BUILDER & LANDSCAPE GARDENER. NO JOB TOO SMALL. A rear door of the vehicle was propped open. Of its owner there was no sign.

Polly frowned. Taking the Fiesta alongside the van, she emerged stiffly to gaze around. The presence of an outsider could be awkward. On the other hand, in an odd way it just might make things easier. If, for privacy's sake, she could persuade Simon's obstructive wife to come out with her in the car, accept neutral ground . . .

To parley on hostile territory was to hand an instant

advantage to the enemy. Everyone knew that. Polly saw no reason to be so obliging, if she could help it.

Approaching the porch, she hoped her voice would hold out. The laryngitis she had advanced as an excuse for staying off work for the past few days was essentially a fiction, but she did have a slight chesty cold which had been making her hoarse if she chattered for too long at a time. It had provided an excellent reason for cutting Simon off when he tried to get argumentative on the phone. Keep him sweating. These were her current tactics, and she had the distinct impression that they were working. The last time he called, Simon had started to sound a little frantic. Polly had enjoyed that.

But she mustn't push it too far. And decidedly she couldn't employ such methods, or anything like them, in her present assignment. This called for subtlety. For the wiles of her own sex, Polly had the healthiest respect. Never underrate the opposition.

A vast, old-fashioned bellpush was fixed to the left of the doorframe. Polly applied pressure.

No sound reached her ears, but she decided to assume that it had rung and await a reply. It was, of course, conceivable that Simon's wife was out for the day. According to Simon, however, she rarely ventured further than the village unless her friend Stephanie drove her into Southweald, which was not more than once a week. Polly had felt it worth taking the chance. She gave the bellpush another thumbing, convinced by now that its mechanism was defunct. When it still produced no response she left the porch and scrunched round to the side of the house in the hope of encountering the builder.

There was no sound of digging or cement-mixing. Now that Polly thought about it, hadn't Simon said something about no start on the work being possible until planning consent had been obtained? So what was the builder doing here at all?

Gates and fences seemed to be in short supply around the

Pettifer residence. Unimpeded, Polly wandered through to the rear garden. Site clearance for the extension had not even begun. The builder, she concluded, must therefore be inside the house, perhaps haggling with Jo over the costs. In the circumstances, the arrival of a third party might be a lot less than welcome. Too bad. Having made the effort, nerved herself finally to take action, Polly had no intention now of withdrawing without a fight.

The patio glass sliding door was, she discovered, open a couple of inches. It glided smoothly the rest of the way, admitting her to a large, square living-room, tastefully decorated and furnished, adorned in several corners with potted plants. Sunlight slanted across two-thirds of the pink-beige carpeting. Nobody was inside the room. Intuition, however, told Polly that it was not part of an empty house. She could feel fresh human vibrations. Crossing the carpet to the inner door, she tugged it open.

'Hi! Anybody home?'

After a moment she stepped boldly into the hall. People, she reflected, really should be more careful. An intruder could have helped himself to anything he fancied, got clean away without raising a sweat. She herself, of course, was intruding. But there was nothing she planned to steal—nothing inanimate, at least—and there was no law, she believed, to forbid one entering private premises as long as no force was used. For the benefit of the builder, she could always announce that she was engaged on market research and wished to interview the lady of the house. She advanced to the foot of the stairs.

'Coo-ee! Anyone around?'

The first-floor landing incorporated several doors, all shut, and further considerable amounts of dead silence. By now thoroughly intrigued, Polly opened one of the doors and peeped inside. It was a main bedroom, equipped with twin beds. She eyed them appraisingly. According to Simon, he and Jo had been living together chastely for some months

. . . since the start of his liaison with Polly, in fact. It might be true. The twin beds were some feet apart.

Polly yearned for it to be true. Everything Simon had been telling her must stand up to scrutiny. Unless he had been levelling with her, she doubted whether she could take it. He was too important to her existence.

Without him, she was nothing. The theatricality of the expression was evident even to herself, and yet it was no more than the simple truth. She was infatuated. That was the reason she was here.

From a corner of the landing a second staircase, steeper than the first, led up to what was plainly an attic room. A thought struck Polly. Perhaps there had been a change of plan. Instead of an extension, the Pettifers could now be considering a conversion job on the roof-space to form extra accommodation at a lower price. Simon had said nothing about this, but then he and Polly had not exactly been exchanging confidences by the dozen just lately. Something told her that Jo and the builder might well be up there at this moment, debating the scheme. Taking a breath, she mounted the stairs.

A solitary door occupied the wall of the miniature landing at the top. With a discreet rap of the knuckles Polly opened it, put her head inside the room.

'Oh!' she exclaimed. 'I do beg your pardon.'

CHAPTER 7

'You did *what*?'

'Went to the house. I was meaning to have a talk with Jo.'

'What about, for God's sake?'

'Simon, be your age. What do you imagine it would have been about?'

Aghast and incredulous, he glared at her. She looked back calmly: ever since the great moment, she had felt cool and dominant, astride of events. Gripping the neck restraint of the driving seat with his left hand, Simon displayed difficulty in getting his breath.

'You must have been crazy to even think about it. How many times have I *implored* you—'

'I've lost count. There's such a thing as overkill, you know. A girl can get sick of being told not to rock the domestic boat. There comes a time when you have to stick an oar in.'

'But to confront Jo like that . . .' Simon paused. '*Would* have been about? You mean you didn't actually speak to her?'

Polly smiled. 'Oh yes. A few words.'

A breeze from the sea rocked the Renault where it sat on the chalk uplands overlooking the coastal roofs of Southweald. The scorching day was expiring with a sigh. Matters climatic were of no immediate concern to Polly. She was watching Simon's features. They had never before revealed so much.

'So?' he demanded. 'What were they?'

'Actually, it was an apology.'

'You apologized to her?'

'Only for intruding. I hadn't meant to poke my nose in on her. Them, I should say.'

Simon's forehead puckered. 'Was Carol there?'

'No, love. It was lunch-time. She was at school.'

'Who, then? Jo's friend Stephanie? She's a blonde, slimly-built—'

'Simon, if you listen I'll tell you. It was nobody female. And he definitely wasn't slim. By simple deduction, I'd say it was this builder you've hired to run up an extension. His van was parked outside.'

Simon relaxed. 'Rod Hawkins. I believe he was calling in. So you simply said sorry and left?'

'That's it. Thought it might be tactful.'

'Not to have gone there in the first place—that might have been still more tactful. Are you quite mad? You could have exploded everything.'

'Funnily enough, that's what I was intending to do. In the event, though, it wasn't necessary.'

He studied her. 'What is it, Poll? What do you have to tell me?'

'Only that they were in bed together. Jo and this Rod Hawkins.'

Simon transferred his gaze impatiently to the ocean. 'That's not funny. I thought we'd driven up here for a serious chat. If you're going to be flippant . . .'

'Who's flipping? I'm telling you the stone-cold truth. There they were together in the attic, under the bedsheets. I think I'd just woken them up.'

In a reflex action, Simon's hand came away from the neck restraint. His body, she saw, was starting to shake. 'I don't believe you.'

'Ask her, then.'

'Don't be ridiculous.'

'Me, ridiculous? Well, if that's the way you feel. Pity, though. There doesn't seem any other way of convincing you.'

Silence held sway inside the car for a considerable time. Bringing out her compact case and lipstick, Polly touched up her lips, glancing at him now and then, satisfied with the effect she had produced. Simon was staring at the dashboard dials as though trying to see a picture in them. His facial skin had turned a dull yellow.

'Jo's not like that,' he mumbled at last. 'She could never . . . She's not made that way.'

Polly returned the cosmetics to her bag. 'I wonder what way she thinks you're made.'

'No need to be cheap,' he said angrily. 'You and me—that's different. We'd worked together, known each other a while before . . . It's different entirely.'

'Oh certainly, my love. It always is.'

He grabbed her by the chin, turned her face towards his. 'You think you're being so smart. Force my hand—that's the plan, isn't it? Get me to over-react. Sorry, Miss Gathercole, but it won't work. I know Jo better than that.'

'Mention Rod Hawkins to her, then, tonight. See how *she* reacts.'

Releasing her chin with a parting thrust, Simon fired the engine and bounced the car back on to the road. He turned left on the coastward descent, foot jammed on throttle. Polly said levelly, 'If it's all the same to you, I'd sooner you didn't kill us both. That won't solve anything.'

He said nothing, kept his foot hard down. The road, poorly made, threw the car about. Polly gripped the sides of her seat, trying not to show fear.

'If you think about it for a moment,' she suggested, watching the bend ahead, 'it gives us a marvellous advantage. See what I'm getting at, Simon? We've got Jo right where we want her. What can she say about us, now?'

'The question never arose, to my knowledge. All I wanted—'

'All you wanted was the well-known bit on the side. Palmy for you, wasn't it? Why bother to change anything?'

'That's hardly fair.'

'No, it hardly isn't. It's hardly fair on me. Did you ever stop to consider that?'

'You only had to opt out.'

'Just like that. So easy.'

For a dangerous second he took his gaze off the road. 'If I'd known you were that deeply—'

'Watch where you're going. The trouble with you, Simon, is that you don't know very much at all. You seem to imagine you can just go on enjoying whatever you fancy and nobody else the worse for it. It doesn't work like that. Sooner or later, you have to make a decision. One way or the other.'

The car yawed. 'You mean, decide between you and my family? We've had this out before. I thought I'd made it absolutely plain—'

'You did your level best. But if this doesn't alter things, what does, for Heaven's sake?'

Biting his lip, Simon took the car erratically into the centre of a road junction and swerved to avoid an oncoming truck. Back on a relatively straight course, he said tautly, 'I've only your word for it that Jo . . . I find it very hard to credit.'

'I see. In other words, I'm a liar?'

'A girl in your position—'

'Suppose we talk about *your* position? It's quite simple. If you don't have it out with Jo, now, tonight, then I shall. Is that clear?'

'I need time to think about it.'

'You've got the rest of the evening. Look, love, all you have to do is tell her you know. After that, it's simply a matter of coming to some amicable—Mind!'

The car slewed into the gutter and back to the crown of the road. Readjusting her posture inside the seat harness, Polly said wrathfully, 'You're driving like a soused teenager. That's all you are—a spoilt brat. If there's something you can't have, you take it out on your toys.'

'Since you've such a low opinion of my character, I wonder you're so anxious to have me all to yourself.'

'Can't help it,' she said quietly, after a pause. 'You're inside my bloodstream, darn it. I'm hooked.'

Emerging on to the coast road, the Renault headed at a canter for the town centre. To their right, the sea sparkled in the late afternoon sun. The promenade was alive with trippers.

'You're making things very difficult for me, Poll.'

'You're making them impossible for yourself.'

'I'm damned if I'm going to march into the house this

evening and say to Jo, Did you sleep with Rod Hawkins today? It's not on.'

'Then I'll do it for you.'

'Careful, Polly.'

'And that's not all. I'll make sure young Carol knows about it.'

Traffic lights ahead switched to amber. Registering the change belatedly, Simon brought the Renault to a shrieking halt yards beyond the white line. Heads turned. The cross-over traffic started to move, brushing the car's nose as it passed. A lorry-driver leaned from his cab window. 'Don't bother leaving space, will you, mate?'

Gripping the wheel, Simon said on a measured key, 'I'd strongly advise you to leave Carol out of this.'

'Frankly, my love, I'm through taking advice from you. From here on, I'm working to my own rules.'

'Polly, I'm warning you.'

'The choice is yours. Have it out with Jo in a civilized way, or risk letting that beloved daughter of yours learn all the gory details . . . and I mean *all*. Not just you and me. The lot. I'm not saying I'd enjoy it. She's just a little kid. But I'll do it, Simon, if I have to. Make no mistake about that.'

CHAPTER 8

Jo had drinks waiting on the trolley. Originally she had laid out the bottles and glasses on the terrace, but without warning—in the space of ten minutes—wisps of inoffensive cloud over the Downs had linked hands and formed up across the entire parade ground of the sky, taking their orders from a moaning wind that had marched on from nowhere, escorted by rain-flecks. Hurriedly retiring indoors, she had called upstairs to Carol that she had better close the attic window while finishing her homework. After that she had concentrated on the meals—fish fingers for Carol, braised steak for Simon, crispbread and an apple for herself—before cleaning out a pair of kitchen cupboards and catching up with a backlog of ironing. By seven, when Carol was watching her favourite TV nature programme, Jo felt that she ached in every muscle she possessed, and yet she was impelled to seek out further tasks, to shun rest. On Simon's eventual arrival at seven-twenty, she abandoned her pastry-making to meet him in the hall.

'Caught me with floury fingers. Have a reasonable sort of day?'

'Mixed.'

'Carol's glued to *Window on Wildlife*. Go and pour yourself a Scotch. I'll be with you in a minute.'

'What are you having?'

'Martini. Not wet, are you?'

'Rain's only just come on. I did a sprint from the car.'

'What happened to summer? An hour ago it was like the tropics.'

'Things can change fast.' Simon went through to the living-room.

Having committed two apple pies to the oven, Jo joined him. Installed on the sofa alongside Carol, he was gazing silently at the screen, apparently captivated by the antics of a leopard cub in an African wilderness. A dry martini had been placed on the low table next to Jo's usual chair, facing the windows. Instead of reclining, she sat stiff-backed on the leading edge of the cushion, nursing her drink, dividing her attention between TV and garden. The latter was now shrinking under a torrent. On screen, the leopard cub was ousted by a commercial for instant soup. Carol reached for the remote control.

'Can we have *Charley and Maud*?'

Simon said absently, 'You didn't like it last week.'

'It might be better this time.'

'I think it's nearly your bedtime.'

'Oh Daddy!'

'Your father's right, Carol. You look sleepy-eyed. Off you go.'

Mutinously, after sundry delaying gambits, Carol retired. Simon switched off the television. Jo glanced across. He raised his eyebrows.

'Something you wanted to see?'

'No. Glad of a bit of silence.' Her gaze returned to the window. 'If you can call it silence, with that downpour. Hark at it.'

'Good thing the extension hasn't been started yet. The footings would have been washed away.'

Jo said nothing.

Simon toyed with his whisky glass. 'Rod Hawkins show up today?'

'Yes. He came along.'

'Just to pick up the plans?'

'He took another look at the site while he was here. Oh, and inspected the drainage.'

'Any problem?'

'Apparently not. He seemed quite satisfied.'

'Find him all right to deal with?'

'Perfectly.'

Jo's position in the chair had not altered during the exchange. Holding his glass steady, Simon manœuvred himself into a horizontal attitude on the sofa with his spine against the end-rest. 'Nothing mentioned about a starting date?'

'Who by?'

'Rod, of course.'

'He has to wait for planning permission.'

'But he must have some idea how long that'll take. And how soon after that—'

'I expect he has, but he said nothing to me about it.' Jo rose. 'Ready for your meal?'

'Give it another five minutes. I'm not that famished.'

Taking the local evening paper from the dresser where Simon had dumped it, Jo studied the front-page headlines with some intensity, dropped it back, walked out to the kitchen. The apple pies had browned nicely. Removing them from the oven, she arranged them side by side on top of the cooker, examined Simon's braised steak on the warmer. After a few moments of total immobility at the centre of the floor, she returned to the living-room. Simon was in the same position, looking down at the carpet. At her re-entry he glanced up.

'I thought you were in a hurry over this annexe?'

'I want it built. For Mother's sake.'

'You don't seem much inclined to talk about it.'

'Everything's been said, for the moment.'

Simon eyed her. 'Quite sure you're happy to give the job to Rod Hawkins?'

'If I wasn't, I'd have said so.'

'Would you?'

'Naturally. There are other builders. Hawkins seems as good as any. Why keep on about him?'

'I was merely inquiring—'

'Well, how about merely dropping the subject? I'd rather like to relax for the evening.'

'Good idea. You do seem a bit tensed up.'

Jo stared at him. Suddenly she burst into tears.

Simon sprang to his feet. 'Hey, what's this? What's this? Did I say something?'

She ran from the room. When she came back, two minutes later, he was at the window, staring out at the rain. Joining him, she stood where her arm was lightly in contact with his. 'Simon, there's something I have to tell you.'

'What is it?'

'I did a stupid thing today. A very stupid thing.'

Simon made no comment; merely waited. 'I made a fool of myself,' she said, enunciating clearly. 'With Rod

Hawkins. I don't quite know how it came about. I can't explain it.'

'What kind of a fool?' Simon's voice was very soft.

'He made a pass at me. I thought he was going to be . . . violent, so I talked my way out of trouble. As I thought. But then he was so nice about it—I lost my head. We went upstairs.' Jo let a moment elapse. 'To Carol's room.'

'Oh Christ.'

'It seemed the . . . the most discreet place. Afterwards I could have killed myself. Him too.' She regarded Simon uncertainly. 'You don't seem all that surprised. Had you guessed?'

Simon gave a shrug. 'Obviously there was something on your mind. Is he important to you?'

'He's nothing! Less than zero. I can't imagine what possessed me. It won't ever happen again. That's something I can say in all honesty.'

Again Simon said nothing. Moving a foot or two clear of him, she gulped faintly and turned. 'I don't know how you feel about it. Can you regard it as a momentary lapse and put it out of your mind? I can't guess. I only know I had to tell you. Couldn't just . . . let it pass.' She paused. 'For one thing, I can't stand the thought now of Rod Hawkins coming round here again. I'd have had to insist on another builder. You'd have wanted to know why.'

'No, I wouldn't.'

Her head jerked. 'So you had guessed?'

'Not exactly. I was informed.'

Jo stared. 'What do you mean?'

He placed a hand on her shoulder, not heavily. 'Somebody spotted you.'

She closed her eyes. Presently, on a dull note, she said, 'Hawkins was right, then. He said he thought someone had peered round the door, said sorry and gone away. I was still asleep at the time. I thought he might have dreamt it. Hoped he had.' Reopening her eyes, she focused them on him. 'Who was it?'

'Polly Gathercole.'

'Oh no! What on earth . . . What was she doing here?'

'Came to have a talk with you.'

'With *me*? A talk? What about?'

Outside, it was raining harder than ever: the light was failing. Reaching past her, Simon hauled on the curtain cord and blotted out the evening. He beckoned.

'Come and sit over here,' he suggested, 'and I'll try to explain.'

Carol awoke feeling troubled. Darkness had assembled at the attic window. She could no longer hear rain. In the oppressive stillness, she fumbled for the switch of her bedside lamp, introduced light into the room at the fourth attempt, blinked at her alarm clock. Twenty minutes to eleven. She had hoped it was morning.

Clambering out of bed, she went outside to the tiny landing. No light was visible from downstairs.

'Mummy?'

A light snapped on: feet started to ascend from the ground floor. 'What is it, darling?'

Her father's voice. Perching on a stair, she waited for him to reach her.

'Couldn't you sleep?'

'I thought it was time to get up.' Carol felt a little foolish.

'Something frighten you?'

'No,' she said defensively.

He smoothed down her hair. 'Come back to your room and I'll tuck you up. Thirsty?'

Carol shook her head. 'I'm hungry, a bit. Can I have a square of chocolate?'

'Just one.' Escorting her back, he added, 'I expect you had a bad dream. Woke you up.'

'I can't remember. Yes, I can.' Recollection surged back.

'I dreamt you and Mummy were both dead. I only had Nan, and she was different. It was horrible.'

'Nightmares,' Simon said briefly, returning to the living-room.

'All right now?'

'Munching chocolate. She'll soon nod off.'

'It'll rot her teeth,' Jo said mechanically.

They sat looking at one another.

'Well,' Simon said presently, 'I guess that about covers it. Anything else you feel I should mention?'

'Before today,' she said slowly, 'I might have suggested an apology. But I'm hardly in a position now to demand that. Admittedly . . .'

'What?'

'Never mind.'

'Tell me.'

'I'm probably being unfair. But I can't help feeling that the reason I went adrift this morning has something to do with the fact that subconsciously I'd been suffering a bit from . . . neglect. If you know what I mean.'

'I've tried to compensate.'

'You've been most attentive. In many ways. Only there's no substitute for . . . It doesn't matter, now. The real question is, do I believe you when you say that Polly means nothing to you on an emotional level? That you're not committed to her?'

Simon puffed his cheeks. 'You've told me that Rod Hawkins was a passing aberration, which I accept. For my part, I can only say I've been trying to cool things with Polly since around March . . . but she's mighty persistent.'

'Of course,' Jo said simply. 'She's fallen for you, like a stone.'

'I've always made it clear to her—'

Jo sighed. 'Why are men so naïve? It always ends the same way. People should know that.'

'Okay,' Simon said huffily, 'I'm green as grass. Point is, how are we going to handle her? She's out to make trouble.'

'She seems to have manufactured quite a bit already,' Jo remarked drily. 'How much is she capable of?'

'I've told you. She wants us to get a divorce. If we don't . . .'

'She'll make things unpleasant for the three of us.' Jo surveyed him. 'Truthfully, how do you feel about it?'

'I don't want anything to change. I like living here, Jo, with you. As for Carol . . . You know how I feel about her.'

'Yes, I think I do.'

'I could never give her up. As for Polly's threats regarding her . . . she lost me from that moment.'

'Speaking for myself,' Jo said on a businesslike note, 'I'm still . . . quite fond of you, Simon. If you want us to stay together, I'm more than willing to make the effort. For Carol's sake in particular. She comes foremost in all this.'

'You bet.'

'Which still leaves Polly. She's got rights, you know. You can't just ignore them.'

'She doesn't have the right to shout about exposing Carol to all kinds of dirt and smear.' Simon's voice became heated. 'You can see the way she's thinking. Aha, she's saying to herself—not only can I make sure that Carol is fully acquainted with her dad's goings-on: I've now got a stranglehold on her mother, into the bargain. Some lever! And it's one she'd be ready to use, given the excuse. I know Polly.'

'You think so?' Jo regarded him speculatively. Simon fidgeted. 'In this case,' she added, rising to pick up the coffee tray, 'I'm inclined to agree with you. Unless Polly gets her way—watch out.'

A wince distorted Simon's features. 'So, what in hell are we going to do about it?'

CHAPTER 9

Polly enjoyed lunching with her brother Clive.

The chance came up infrequently, but when it did they got along famously. Although they had gone separate ways since childhood, they had kept in touch and were now, if anything, even closer than when they were united in hostility to their stepmother at home in Sheffield. Polly had been first to quit. At eighteen, she had stormed south to make a life of her own; but she hadn't abandoned young Clive, who was fifteen at the time. In due course, at Polly's urging, Clive had obtained parental backing for a computer course which finally had won him independence from the stifling atmosphere of No. 48, Dale Crescent, and placed him on the bottom rung of the ladder which had since hoisted him to a position of trust in the Northern and Midlands Investment Corporation (NAMIC). Clive liked and respected his sister. She continued to feel, in an odd way, protective towards him, while simultaneously regarding him as something of a father-confessor. In the latter category, he was all she had.

'So,' she remarked, plastering a wholemeal bread roll contentedly with low-fat spread, 'you're down here to chase up a client?'

'Four clients.'

'Golly. NAMIC must be doing well.'

'We survive,' Clive agreed with some complacency. 'While I'm hitting the South Coast, I might rustle up an extra spot of business, too. Depends on contacts. Be around a week or so, at least. What would you say, Dolly, to a night out?'

'I'd say, Hullo, Night Out, greetings and welcome. He doesn't call often.'

'We might fix up a foursome.'

Polly looked at him fondly across the cutlery. He was a large young man, dense-browed, every inch the thrusting executive. From nobody else would she have accepted the corruptions of her first name: it dated from the nursery, where Clive had found it less taxing to formulate a D than a P. 'Know anyone around here?' she asked.

'Nobody under sixty. I was hoping you might be able to fetch someone along.'

Polly reflected. 'There's Irene, in Frozen Foods. She might fancy a bit of a fling.'

'Persuade her. I hope she's warmer than her work.'

'From what I know of her,' Polly said significantly, 'she can be quite hot stuff. Anyway, you're the great melter-down of iced exteriors, aren't you? So you're always telling me.'

Clive threw her a wink. 'I'm having the Florida cocktail and the fish. Same for you?' Leaning back, he scanned the somewhat antiseptic appointments of the Harbour Grill, humming to himself, before launching himself forward again to inspect his sister with a solicitous eye. 'Last time you wrote, you were having a spot of hassle with this bloke you were knocking around with. What's the update on that?'

'Working out quite nicely.'

'Married, isn't he?'

'We don't let small things like that stand in our path.'

'Heaven forbid. All the same,' Clive said acutely, keeping her under scrutiny, 'they can tend to create problems, now and then. Are you telling me, Dolly, it's all roses, this relationship?'

'There *were* a few little snags,' Polly admitted. 'In fact, to tell you the honest truth, I'd begun to wonder if I was flogging a dead horse, up until recently. There's been an improvement now.'

'Horse made a fast recovery?'

'Shall we say—' she inspected the varnish on her finger-nails—'the rider's found a new set of spurs?'

'Good for you. How's the diet going?'

'Lost three pounds.'

'Since when?'

'Since I started. I'm not telling you when that was. You thank your stars, young man, you don't have to spend your whole life watching the calories.' Polly gazed longingly at the remaining two-thirds of her bread roll before sweeping it resolutely aside. 'It's not so hard, now I've got the incentive.'

'The recovering horse?'

'That's right.'

'What's his name?'

'Simon. We did go through a bad patch, but I reckon things are going to work out. First, though, there's a bit of action I might have to take. I'm not sure. It depends.'

Clive rubbed his nose. 'Action?'

'Don't look so suspicious. I'm not figuring to bump off his wife or something. It's more a question of . . . moral persuasion.'

'Oh yes? Best of luck.'

'And if you think that shows I'm living in cloud cuckoo land, you've another think coming. For once in my life, as it so happens, I'm holding all the cards.'

'You mean you can turn the screws on him?'

'Both of them. Don't ask me to spill any more trade beans—not just now. I can explain better after tomorrow night.'

'Why tomorrow night?'

'Because that's when we're due to have it out, the three of us. They've asked me over,' Polly enlarged, 'to discuss the whole thing: presumably they're under the impression there's some kind of compromise we can arrive at. I'm afraid I've got news for them.' She patted her hair. 'Little Polly's going to be in the driving seat—make a change, won't it? I'm quite looking forward to the occasion.'

'I'll be fascinated to hear about it.'

'Give you a call,' she promised. 'Wednesday morning,

first thing. Comprehensive news bulletin. I'll let you know then about the foursome, as well. Let's have your phone number and I'll ring before nine.'

Although senior by five months, Lynda Ross had so far made less physical headway than Carol and was of an even more unassertive disposition. Carol felt at ease with her. Some of the others at the village school were hard to get on with: they were so rough. Carol was glad that Lynda's mother and her own were friends, too. Without Auntie Steph and her Metro, Carol would have had to rely on the school bus, which she didn't fancy at all.

Plucking a rosebud from the solitary bush in her friend's front garden, fronting the village main street, Carol wrinkled her nose over the embryonic petals. 'We've got somebody coming tonight,' she volunteered.

'Who?'

'I don't know. Somebody from where Daddy works.' Carol's nose acquired deeper corrugations. 'I've got to go to bed early.'

'I'm staying up,' Lynda said humbly. 'Mummy said I could. There's a film about ballet on Channel Five.'

Carol released a wail. 'I knew I'd miss something. There's always a film on when I—'

'Tea up, girls.' Stephanie Ross, ash-blonde and slender, emerged from the cottage, shielding her eyes against the glare. 'Come and have it, Carol, because I promised I'd get you home by six. Worked up an appetite?'

'Auntie Steph, I'm going to miss the ballet film.'

'Oh dear. Why?'

'I have to go to bed early. We're having a visitor.'

'Bad luck. Tell you what. We'll video it for you, then you can see it when you next come to tea. How's that?'

'Thank you very much.' It wasn't the same as seeing it contemporaneously with Lynda, but Carol was a dutiful child when it came to expressions of gratitude, and a second-hand viewing was undoubtedly better than none. After doing justice to Stephanie's salmon and cucumber sandwiches, she and Lynda played elasticated tennis in the rear garden until five to six, when Stephanie drove her home. Setting her down at the gate, Stephanie peeped along the drive.

'Still no start, I see, on the extension for your Nan.'

'We're having a different builder,' Carol explained, retrieving her school bag from the rear seat.

'Oh? Your mother didn't tell me that. Was the first one no good?'

'I don't know.' Nobody told Carol anything. She paddled through life, she sometimes felt, across a lake of pure ignorance. 'It might be built in the autumn,' she added, in a bid to re-establish some authority.

'You'll like it, won't you, when your Nan's living next door?'

Carol nodded, although she had mixed feelings about the prospect. For some reason, her father's attitude towards Nan always made her feel vaguely uneasy. It was better, really, when there was distance between them and they only talked on the phone.

She found her mother vacuum-cleaning the living-room floor. It was the kind of strident, inhospitable homecoming she especially disliked. However, after a few minutes the Hoover was switched off and speech became feasible. Stowing the appliance in the hall cupboard, Jo smiled cheerfully at her daughter.

'Enjoy yourself?'

'I had two pieces of Victoria sponge.' Carol decided on a last-ditch attempt. 'Lynda's going to watch the ballet film. Can I—'

'Sorry, darling, but I want you in bed by seven-thirty sharp. You know we've got a visitor.'

'All right.' Carol resigned herself to the inescapable. 'Can I read in bed?'

'Fifteen minutes. No longer. Then you must go straight off to sleep. We and our . . . guest have a lot to talk about. Promise you'll lie down at a quarter to eight?'

'Promise.' What a fuss was being made about this silly visitor. 'What will you be talking about?' she inquired, to show interest. 'Is it something to do with the supermarket?'

'In a way,' said Jo. 'Fairly important, but very boring. You wouldn't want to listen to a word of it.'

At seven-twenty, Polly collected her Fiesta from the garage behind the apartment block and brought it round to the parking area at the front.

Returning to the flat, she substituted a cream, pleated-cotton skirt for the pale pink satin trousers she had originally opted for, muted the shade of her lipstick, pinned her tawny hair back behind her ears. Assessing the general effect in the long mirror inside her lobby, she decided that another eight pounds or so would have to come off before she could safely adopt any other style for everyday usage. Leaving the flat a second time, she double-locked the outer door and clattered downstairs for the exercise. On the third-floor landing, an elderly woman inserting her latchkey into a door turned arthritically to investigate.

'*Good* evening, Miss Gathercole. Off out again?'

'Hi, Miss Brent.' Nosey cow. Sweetly intent on monitoring all residential activities. 'Yes, another wild night of debauchery. No stopping us, is there?'

She earned herself a frosted smile before descending out of sight. In a way, she thought, heading for ground level, she wouldn't be sorry to abandon the flat, for all its advantages. Most of the time, anonymity was not only possible but inevitable: ill-lit as the common parts were, few residents were inclined to loiter outside their apartments, observing the passing traffic. On the other hand, every block tended to have its Miss Brent. There was much to be said in favour of a house in its own ground, shielded by brick, timber and foliage, an entity in its own right. Driving off in the Fiesta, Polly allowed herself to dream a little.

CHAPTER 10

'Sugar, Miss Gathercole?'

'Call me Polly. Everybody does.'

'I had a favourite aunt called Polly.' Hearing the contrived matiness in her own remark, Jo despised herself. It was that or open hostility, and the latter alternative seemed uncalled for. 'Actually she was a great-aunt. She lived to be ninety-eight.'

'Fancy.' The tone of Polly's response was one of polite non-interest. She had, Jo noted, a North Country accent: Lancs or Yorks? When it came to regional dialects, Jo was on shaky ground. The same applied to tightly-strung social occasions. For the moment, she was on her own. Simon had clammed up. No help to be expected, yet, from that quarter.

Taking the objective view, Jo could see what he had found anatomically alluring about his chief checkout supervisor, in whom voluptuousness had yet to yield place to obesity. What did puzzle her was how Simon, himself a fastidious elocutionist, could have endured for more than a few weeks the faintly rasping vocal delivery which was the most distinctive part of Polly's overall personality. Men were beyond comprehension.

'Sugar?' she repeated, hovering with the bowl.

'Better not.' Their visitor sent a low-powered smile on a circular tour of the room. 'Well, isn't this nice? Grandstand view of the Downs and everything. You ought to keep a pony out there.' Jo, her manner implied, was wilfully neglecting her obligations by failing to do so. 'Mind you, they're a lot of work, horses. All got enough to do, haven't we? Without adding to it. We're kept busy, I know that. Right, Simon? If it's not tills going on the blink, it's customers writing their cheques wrong or trying to use other stores' chargecards. Never a dull minute. Isn't that right, Simon?'

He sent her a brooding look, nodded briefly, drank from his cup.

'Poor old Simon. The buck stops with him. He must spend half his life mediating.'

'That's the impression I get,' said Jo.

'You hear quite a lot about it, I expect.' Polly turned the smile, now nuclear-powered, back on to her hostess. 'Men in Simon's position—they like to unburden themselves, don't they? D'you find that? They need an outlet.'

'Stress,' Jo said desperately, 'can get to anyone, I imagine. Male or female.' Retreating to her chair, she sat stiffly on the edge of it, circulating her coffee with the sugar-spoon. 'It can make them do things they . . . wouldn't otherwise consider.'

'You're so right! I agree with you, Jo.'

'In Simon's case, I know he's been under a lot of strain.'

'I'm sure he has.'

'Which is really what we wanted to talk to you about. You see, Polly—'

'Oh, I understand the position. Perfectly. I wouldn't have come if I didn't.'

Simon glanced across. Avoiding his eye, Jo said hurriedly, 'That's fine. Things are so much easier if you can discuss them in a sensible way. Don't you think?'

'Oh, I'm all for a slice of common sense.'

'In that case . . .' Jo took a steadying breath. 'We might as well get down to basics. Obviously you know why we invited you here this evening . . .'

Polly adjusted the smile to low wattage, and remained silent.

'We both feel we owe you an explanation. Simon and I, we've quite a . . . a sound marriage, actually. I mean, we do see more or less eye to eye, most of the time. It's not as if we're always at each other's throats.'

'You're an easy person to get on with, Jo. I can see that.'

'What I'm saying is—'

'What she's saying,' interrupted Simon, raising his head suddenly, 'is that our relationship hasn't fallen apart. As I've been trying to explain to you, Polly, for quite some while. There's no question of Jo and I splitting up. It's not on.'

'You have mentioned it a few times, lately.'

'Not just lately. If you recall, right from the outset—'

'It's not likely to have slipped my mind.'

The smile loitered on Polly's lips, but it had deserted her eyes. Fighting down her inner dismay, Jo took up the running. 'It's no excuse, now, for Simon to say that he warned you from the start. I can see that. It wasn't fair on you. At the same time, that's no reason—'

'Quite honestly, Jo, I'm not asking for reasons or excuses. I'm just here to help clarify the situation. It could do with a bit of sorting out, wouldn't you say?'

'I think the situation itself is plain enough. What concerns me—us—is the effect on yourself. This is why—'

'Don't worry about me. I can look after myself. Not that I reckon on having to, to be perfectly frank about it.' Polly beamed from one to the other. 'The point is, you see, I'm in love with Simon and he loves me. So it would be daft, wouldn't it, to chuck it all up, just for the sake of appearances? It wouldn't be right.'

Jo breathed in again, gaining control of her voice. 'Don't you think it goes deeper than that?'

'Oh, a lot. It's complicated, isn't it, Jo? There's the other side of the coin to be taken into account. We mustn't forget.'

'I don't think I quite . . .'

'What are you driving at, Polly?' Simon spilt coffee over the back of his hand. Tugging out a handkerchief, he mopped up while continuing to glare at her.

Polly remained placid. 'I wouldn't have thought you needed reminding. And I certainly don't wish to stir things up, unnecessarily. But in case you *have* forgotten, this isn't my first visit to your house . . . right? I've been here before. And I saw something.'

There was a short silence.

Jo leaned against the side of her chair. 'You saw me in bed, with another man.'

'I'm not criticizing, Jo. Don't get me wrong. Hardly for me to pass judgement, is it? But I can draw conclusions.'

'And what conclusion have you drawn?'

'Well, I mean. Do I need to spell it out?'

Consigning her cup and saucer to the tray, Jo resettled herself in an upright posture and folded her hands on her lap. 'What happened that morning, Miss Gathercole, has been gone into fully and disposed of. Simon understands perfectly. It was an isolated incident that meant nothing. There's no more to be said about it.'

'Does Simon see it that way?'

'Ask him.'

'As a matter of fact, I already have. And the feeling I got was that he was shattered, quite honestly.'

'But now that he's had time to adjust . . .'

'You do agree, then, it's a new situation? One that calls for adjustment?'

'Not in the way you're clearly trying to imply.'

'All I'm suggesting,' Polly said reasonably, 'is that, as things stand, you've no special claim on Simon, any more than anyone else. Come on, Jo. You've got to admit that.'

'Don't be so crass, woman.' Simon almost spat the words from his armchair. 'One passing indiscretion doesn't wipe out years of marital stability—you know that.'

'I do?'

'If you don't, it's time you took a few lessons. People who can't accept that there are such things as tolerance, forgiveness—'

'All right, Simon,' Jo said quietly.

'It's not all right. Polly's behaving like an adolescent.' He turned to her. 'Can't you see? Hasn't it got through to you that Jo and I intend to be responsible about this? It's not just us. Others are involved. You don't simply—'

'Leave it, Simon. That's enough.'

'It's all right, Jo. I can look after myself.' Polly's bland insinuation that the two females in the room were at one in their opposition to male intransigence sent a feeling of helplessness through Jo's bloodstream. She knew there was something she ought to say, but what was it? Meanwhile, Polly had turned her entire attention to Simon. 'Maybe I'm not such a dimwit as you seem to think. You've got duties as parents—that's what you mean, right? You're worried about Carol.'

'We'd be pretty unnatural if we weren't. A child of nine—'

'Impressionable age,' Polly said knowingly. 'Any emotional upset at a time like this . . .'

'I'm glad you appreciate the fact.'

'Oh, I'm very aware of it. Very much aware. It could scar her for life. Wouldn't take much, would it? A word or two in her ear. *Look here, Carol, Daddy's been fooling around with this woman, so he and Mummy—*'

'Careful, Polly. Just you mind what you're saying.'

'I'm not actually saying it, am I? Not yet. I hope I never have to. I wouldn't want to be accused of warping a child's personality.'

'There's an easy way of avoiding that.'

'Ah, but then you must remember, I've my own position to protect.' Polly gazed at them, bright-eyed. 'I want you to be quite clear, both of you, about what I'm capable of. I don't want there to be any misunderstanding. If it came to the point—and I'm not saying it will—but if it did, there's a hell of a lot I could say to young Carol, concerning either of you. As long as you're under no misapprehension about that.'

Simon made a very slight movement in his chair. 'Are you threatening us?'

'I'm dishing out a friendly warning.'

'We don't have to talk in this vein, surely?' Jo's intervention sounded in her own ears like a bleat from a hillside. 'If we all approach the problem like adults—'

'There's no *problem*, Jo,' said Polly kindly. 'It's all cut and dried, to my mind. You're faced with two choices. You can agree to split up, in which case Carol loses her dad but keeps some of her illusions. Or you can be obstructive. In which case, I might have to take the gloves off. Messy for Carol—very unfortunate. Avoidable, though.' She sat back comfortably, cup in hand.

'Well? Which is it to be?'

By jamming one ear against the pillow and blocking the other with her palm, Carol could drown out seventy per cent of the vocal decibels drifting up from below; but there was nothing she could do about the remainder. Turning over, she hauled the bedclothes over her head, lay there a few moments half-stifled by the heat. Useless. Still the voices came through, distorted but insistent, a medley of pitch and tone. Were they playing cards? She had heard her father talk in that way when he was losing.

Emerging from the cocoon, she swung her legs out of bed.

Although the sun had set, the afterglow continued to illuminate the attic. The stairs, however, were almost in darkness. Thumbing the light switch, Carol gathered the hem of her dressing-gown carefully about her calves and descended to the first-floor landing.

From there, the sounds were amplified, ugly. She had never heard her father shout with such vehemence, such hostility. Nor her mother. Was it her mother? It was a woman's voice, but it carried overtones unfamiliar to Carol

. . . triumph, spite, menace . . . and there was a different sound to the words. Carol gripped the banister. Nothing that was going on downstairs, behind that closed door, was within her experience. She didn't pretend to understand. All she knew was that she didn't like it.

Abandoning caution, she took the rest of the stairs in five leaps, then trotted along the hall to the living-room door.

When, with a thumping heart, she pushed it open, the first thing she saw was the distortion of her mother's face. On her feet next to her armchair, Jo was clutching the backrest while glaring across the room at the visitor, who —as Carol by now had guessed—was a woman. Quite a young woman, not unlike Stella, the main character in the current TV serial which Carol was allowed to watch every Wednesday. Like Stella, she had very dark hair cut in a frontal fringe and falling past the back of her ears; and like Stella she looked glamorous, in the way that Carol had come to associate with the small screen. There were other similarities with television. To Carol's eyes, the scene was reminiscent of a studio confrontation which had got a little out of hand. Her father, although seated, was not relaxed. Leaning forward, he was uttering words to which the visitor was paying cool and faintly amused attention . . . just like Stella, when her family started to get on at her. Slipping out of Carol's grasp, the door swung wide open to connect sharply with a corner of the dresser. All three adults jerked round.

'Well well!' cried the visitor. 'Look who we've got here.'

Jo ran across. 'Carol, I thought I told you—'

'Let her stay. Why not? This involves her, just as much as—'

'Shut up, you bitch!'

Carol stood dumbstruck, less at the words he had used than at the venom in her father's voice. Her mother grabbed her by the shoulders. 'Go back to bed at once. You're a very disobedient girl.'

Carol's lip quivered. 'I can't sleep. I can hear you all talking.'

The effect of this relatively mild accusation surpassed her intentions. Her father leapt from his chair; her mother's grip on her shoulder-blades tightened painfully. 'You mean you heard what was said? Have you been listening?'

The glamorous visitor, now the only one remaining seated, spoke up from her corner. 'If she's taken in this much, she might as well stop and hear the rest. Hi, Carol. Listen, I'm a friend of your dad's. We're having a little friendly argument, that's all. I'll explain what it's about. Your daddy and I—'

'Get the child out of here!'

In a reflex response to Simon's shout, Jo spun her daughter back towards the door. From behind them, Polly raised her own voice. 'Don't let them push you around, Carol my love. You've a right to know. Your mother—'

The sentence ended strangely. It was like a telephone message cut off by a fault on the line. As she was bundled out into the hall, Carol saw nothing: she heard clearly, however, the sounds that accompanied and followed the abrupt cessation of the visitor's voice. Like soft sneezes, they were, and then a thud, as if the sneezer had lost balance and fallen against something. Impelled back to the stairs by her mother's inflexible hands, Carol came dejectedly to terms with the fact that she would never be given the chance to decipher the mystery. It was, she knew instinctively, destined to remain locked away inside one of those impenetrable adult strongboxes to which children could never hope to obtain the key. Submitting to the inevitable, she plodded up five stairs before turning.

'Will you be talking much longer?'

'We'll try to cut it short, darling.' Her mother's voice was wobbly. 'I'm sorry we disturbed you. There's a small disagreement we're trying to settle—nothing for you to bother your head about. I expect you found it all a bit hard to understand?'

'I couldn't hear what you were saying. It was just the voices.'

'Very thoughtless of us.' Carol received a sudden hug from her mother. Tell you what. If you run upstairs now and climb back into bed, I'll be up in a little while with some hot chocolate. How does that sound?'

'And a biscuit?'

'All right—special treat. And don't pay any heed to us silly old grown-ups downstairs. We're not worth bothering about.'

Silence embraced the living-room. Hesitating at the door, Jo embarked on a marathon intake of breath, struggled to compose herself from the fingertips inwards. Presently, with a resolute twist of the door-handle, she went inside.

At first the room seemed empty. For a moment she entertained the hope that Polly had cooled down, seen reason, left the house to be helped back into the Fiesta by Simon. But there wouldn't have been time. She would have met them in the hall. Unless they had left by the patio door, which in fact was still locked from within. Mystified, she stepped further into the room and caught sight of Simon's left shoe.

'What's going on?' she asked sharply.

The shoe buckled as the rest of him rose into view from behind the armchair where Polly had been sitting. His face shocked her. The skin was mud-coloured; the mouth hung slack. The eyes were vacant. She went forward to touch his sleeve.

'What were you doing down there? Where's Polly?'

Simon looked dazedly across his shoulder. 'There.'

Jo stared at him. Advancing another pace, she peered round the side of the armchair. Polly seemed to be asleep in the angle of the walls. Jo frowned.

'Is she tight? I didn't realize she'd been drinking.'

'Not tight. Dead.'

'Oh, don't be absurd.'

'Her neck's floppy. She bashed her head as she went back.'

'You're imagining it. People don't . . .'

Jo's voice tailed off. She moved tentatively closer, half-expecting the young woman's eyes to reopen, gaze back at her. Polly, however, remained to all appearances heavily in slumber. Jo put out a hand. Simon spoke hoarsely from overhead.

'Don't touch her!'

'Why not? We have to find out whether—'

'Not necessary. Surely you can see? She's had it.'

Feeling giddy, Jo drew back. Hoisting herself up from her knees, she stood regarding the motionless figure through a mental haze. 'In that case,' she heard herself declare, 'we must call the doctor. Do we have his number handy?'

'What good will that do?'

'You have to call in the doctor. Don't you? Doesn't he have to establish the cause of death or something?'

'We know what caused it. I hit her. She fell out of the chair on to her head.'

'You must have struck her terribly hard.'

'Of course I did. I was trying to protect Carol.'

'You didn't have to be quite so violent.'

Side by side, they stared down at the hunched body in the corner. It's like the start of a play, Jo thought dreamily. Act One, Scene One: the study of the Colonel's residence. Backstage, partly behind the desk, the legs of a recumbent figure . . . She took a hold of herself. 'If we're not going to call a doctor, at least we should contact the police.'

'Let's wait a bit.'

'Why? They'll have to be notified. What's the point of delay?'

'Jo, come over here.'

Simon led her to the window. 'I'm in a spot,' he told her. The dazed manner was starting to ebb: he was talking more coherently. 'We both are. It's vital that we think very carefully about this.'

'What on earth are you getting at? It was accidental. Provided we explain just what took place—'

'What if they don't believe us?'

'Why shouldn't they?'

'Use some gumption. Think about it. Why was Polly here with us tonight?'

Jo blinked at him. 'We don't have to give chapter and verse on that. We can say it was purely a social call. Who's to know?'

'Rod Hawkins, for one.'

'What are you talking about?'

Simon shook her. 'I'm talking about facts. Polly saw the two of you in bed in the attic—right? And Hawkins saw Polly. She told me. He sat up in bed and their eyes met. So, the chances are he'll remember her. He's got a sharp eye for the ladies, it seems.'

'Supposing he did? He wouldn't say anything. He's not the gossiping type.'

'Care to bet on it? If word of this gets out,' Simon said deliberately, 'and Hawkins reads about it and does identify her from the photos, he'll quite likely put two and two together and realize the two events might be connected. He might go to the police. They could start asking questions.'

'The most they can do is charge you with criminal negligence . . .'

'They can charge me just as easily with manslaughter. And assuming they dug up some of the background, they could conceivably make it something worse.'

'You're fantasizing.' Jo groped for arguments to head him off. 'They'd never . . . I can't think it would work out like that. Suppose the worst did happen and you were accused of causing her death. Once it came to court and we described the circumstances . . .'

'They'd still only have our word for it. And that's not all.' Pacing away to the dresser, Simon drummed his fingers on its polished surface, came back. 'If I'm brought to trial, I can kiss goodbye to my job with Granger's.'

'So what? If they're petty enough to—'

'Or any other job in that line. Convicted killers aren't exactly in hot demand for managerial posts in supermarkets. I'd be branded goods.'

'You'd find something else,' Jo said uncertainly.

'Is that a chance you're willing to take? Out of a job. Debts piling up. Forced to sell the house. No flat for your mother. Carol going hungry . . .'

'You're putting the worst possible case. I don't see it need come to that.'

'And to cap it all,' Simon added, as if she hadn't spoken, 'we'd be defeating the original aim of the entire exercise. In order to explain what led up to Polly's death, we'd have to describe how we were trying to keep the seamy side of things from Carol. The moment we do that, it all gets aired in public. Press stories, TV reports—the works.'

Jo gazed at him in horror. 'Surely it wouldn't arouse as much interest as that?'

'Are you serious? The media would have us for breakfast. What sort of effect is that going to have on Carol?'

Jo went and sank on to the footstool facing the TV screen. From there, the still figure of Polly was hidden. At this moment she was not thinking of Polly. Other images were swimming into her mind. The front pages of tabloid newspapers. Screaming headlines. COURT HEARS OF 'TRIANGLE' KILLING. CHILD OF DEATH HOUSE PARENTS TAKEN INTO CARE . . .

She looked back at Simon. 'What did you have in mind?'

CHAPTER 11

Carol was lying propped up on an elbow in bed, reading. Jo offered her the chocolate. 'Drink it while it's hot. After that you can read for another five minutes, then you must lie down.'

'Has the visitor gone?'

'Yes. She's gone.'

Jo stayed with her daughter while she drank the chocolate. Then she planted a kiss on her cheek, said good night and returned downstairs. Simon was tying the final knots in the cord around the plastic dustbin-liners in which he had encased the body. At Jo's re-entry he glanced up from the floor alongside the armchair where he was kneeling.

'Did you get it down her?'

'She drank the lot.'

'How long will it take?'

'Five or ten minutes. I only gave her a half. That ought to keep a child asleep for ten hours.'

Simon grunted. 'Lucky you had some in the house. I didn't know you'd been taking sleeping pills.'

'After this,' said Jo, low-voiced, 'I'll be swallowing a few more.'

With a quick look at the shiny-black sausage which now occupied the place where Polly had fallen, she turned her back. 'What's the next step?'

'Find her car keys. They'll be in her bag.'

Polly's mini-portmanteau of white synthetic leather sat on the armchair. Releasing its jaws, Jo rummaged in a lucky dip of contents until her fingers made contact with a key on a holder shaped like a small padlock. Fishing it out, she passed it across. Simon gave it a swift look.

'That's the one to her flat. Have another look.'

'Nothing else here,' she reported presently. 'Spray, compact, paper tissues . . . A lot of other junk, but no key.'

'Tried her purse?'

'I can't see one.'

'She always carried cash.' Simon rose irritably to join her. 'There has to be a purse.'

'You find one.'

He made a vain search. Finally he upended the bag, scattering Polly's possessions . . . among them, a square-print photograph of himself, taken by Jo a year previously. Both of them pretended not to see it. Having sifted through the medley, Simon sat back on his heels with a hiss.

'Don't say it was in her pocket . . .'

'You'll have to look.'

'For Christ's sake. Once was bad enough. I can't do it twice.'

Jo surveyed the heap of belongings in silence. 'If you're determined to go through with this,' she said, 'you've no choice. You've got to be able to drive her car.'

She made to stand up. Seeking support with her left hand on the seat of the armchair, she felt something solid against her fingers. Delving deeper, she produced a purse from the space between chairframe and cushion. Simon snatched it out of her hand.

'Got it!' he said in triumph, yanking a key from inside. 'Thank God for that. Put the purse back in her bag, with the rest of the stuff.'

Mechanically Jo did as she was told. Meanwhile Simon left the room. She was unaware of this until she turned to put a question and found herself alone with the plastic package on the floor. Rising in panic, she escaped to the hall. Simon was emerging from the downstairs cloakroom, clad in his golfing anorak of dark cotton and unfurling the peaked cap which he carried in one of its zip pockets. At sight of her he raised a warning finger.

'Keep your voice down,' he whispered. 'Carol might not have crashed out yet.'

'I'd be surprised if she hasn't. How about gloves?'

'Gloves?'

'Fingerprints. The car. Shouldn't you take precautions?'

Wordlessly he went through to the kitchen, to reappear a moment later tugging on the rubber hand-protectors that Jo kept on a hook above the sink. They were pale pink. 'A bit conspicuous,' he acknowledged, smoothing the rubber about his fingers, 'but it's only while I'm in the car. I'll take them off on the way back.'

'We've already handled her bag. And the purse.'

'Fetch me a damp cloth.'

Back inside the living-room, they set to work on Polly's belongings. Simon dealt with the purse and car keys while Jo went methodically through the bag's contents, polishing the casings of the powder compact and lipstick, cleaning the hand-mirror, the bag itself. Each item she returned carefully to the lined interior. Adding the purse, Simon stood up.

'I'll take it out to the car.'

While he was gone, Jo withdrew to the kitchen and sat beside the refrigerator. Listening numbly to its industrious hum as it got on with its job, she found herself shivering despite the warmth of the night. At Simon's stealthy return she dragged herself off the stool.

'Can you manage by yourself?'

'No problem. But I'd like the doors held open.'

Stationing herself outside the living-room door, which tended to drift back, Jo held it wide with one hand while pressing herself to the wall. Presently there were scuffing sounds as Simon, burdened, came through. Trying not to look, she preceded him along the hall and opened the porch door to give him a clear passage out on to the drive. The scuffing became a scrunching, intimidatingly loud in the night stillness, until Simon reached the opened hatchback of the Fiesta, turned, shrugged off the load. It fell with a muffled thump into the loading bay. To expand the available space, he had lowered the rear seat-backs. Straightening with a gasp, he reached up and hauled on the hatchback door, which fell heavily on to its catch but failed to lock. Cursing under his breath, Simon did it twice more: at the third attempt the door was secured.

'Okay,' he said softly, looking back towards the porch. 'Get back inside.'

'How will you—'

'I'll manage. Just stay here with Carol. I'll be as fast as I can.'

Her head was one vast ache.

Returning from her seventh ascent of the stairs to check on Carol—soundly asleep on her side, with an arm dangling over the edge of the mattress—Jo saw from the kitchen wall-clock that it was approaching one-thirty. Three hours since she had watched the tail-lights of the Fiesta through the gateway and into the lane. By now, the clock had a sneer on its digital face. Everything she looked at seemed to be half-concealing a derisory smile.

At midnight she had made tea. The cup remained at her elbow, its contents undisturbed. She had tried having the radio on softly: all that was obtainable was idiot music and gobbling voices, distorted by rival signals. The day's newspapers lay untouched.

Well before midnight, she had thought she heard the engine-note of the Fiesta returning. She had waited for what seemed to be twenty minutes, but Simon had not reappeared. Eventually she had gone out to the porch. The drive was empty.

Since then she had heard nothing. Sometimes, with the breeze in the right quarter, the sound of cars in the village drifted across the fields to the house; tonight there was not a murmur.

At two o'clock she made coffee.

She was setting out the tray with painstaking attention to detail when her ears picked up the vibrancies in the hall. She opened the kitchen door. The figure approaching, silhouetted by the porch light, was hunch-shouldered and moving laboriously, like a distance runner struggling to the tape after ten thousand metres against a headwind. Holding the door, she helped him through, guided him to the stool.

'You've been an *eternity*. Did something go wrong?'

He shook his head, pointed to the tray. 'I could use some of that.'

Silently she handed him a cupful, black, sweetened, which he swallowed in voracious gulps. 'Apart from everything else,' he said, passing the cup back with gestures indicating that she should refill it, 'I've walked about sixty miles. Six, anyhow.'

Jo leaned against the worktop, pressing a palm to the side of her head where the throb was busiest. 'Did it . . . all go to plan?'

Having drunk half of the second cupful, he nursed the cup and saucer on his knee for a few moments before nodding decisively, as if sanctioning a new line in canned beans after stringent appraisal. 'I left the car back in her garage before going up to the flat. Nobody saw me. I'm positive. It was pitch dark inside the building and I didn't use any of the lights.'

'Somebody might have looked out. Spotted you opening her door . . .'

'Nobody did,' he said firmly. 'By the time I got there it was close on midnight. Every resident in the entire block was either still glued to the screen or else fast asleep. All I had to do was step inside, dump the handbag on a chair . . .'

'In the lobby?'

'No, I took it right through to the lounge. Put it down on a leather chair just inside the door, as if she'd left it there on her way into the kitchen. Then I—'

'Keys?'

'I stowed both of them back inside her purse. Car and apartment.'

'Then you left? Did anybody see you go?'

'I tell you,' Simon said impatiently, 'I came and went like a ghost. Believe me, I'd know if I hadn't. In that place, you can't mistake if you're being overlooked. I'm pretty familiar with it by now.'

'I expect you are.' Jo stared down sightlessly at her interlocked fingers. 'Then what? Did you get a bus?'

'At that time of night? I walked a mile or two up the London road, then thumbed an HGV driver. He took me as far as the West Challerton turn-off and I hiked again from there. Four miles, if it's a yard. Not a glimmer anywhere. At times I was nearly in the ditch.'

'How about that driver? He might remember you, in the event of—'

'Who'd be likely to ask?'

'If they really started making inquiries,' she said doggedly, wincing as the throb became momentarily a stab inside her skull. 'Don't the police put out appeals sometimes? Any driver who picked up a hitch-hiker in a certain area, on a particular night . . .'

'All he'd have seen of me,' Simon said with assurance, 'is a bespectacled face under a close-fitting cap, in the half-dark.' Producing a red case from a pocket of the anorak, he tapped it with his knuckles. 'I wore these the whole time . . . same as when I used to visit Polly. The long-range ones I use for night-driving. You've said yourself how they change my appearance.'

'That lorry-driver may have exceptionally sharp eyes. Anyhow, there are other ways of identifying people. Voice prints . . .'

'Calm down, will you?' Rising stiffly, Simon limped over to the cooker, turned, propped himself against it while gazing at her. 'Don't you see? There's not going to be any reason for the police to ask about a *man* hitching a lift. If the question arises at all, they're going to be inquiring about a woman. Surely that's obvious?'

'To us, it may be. But there are times,' Jo said with the compulsiveness of a patient picking at a scab, 'when it can be hard to put yourself in the place of an outsider. We're assuming that they'll think she drove herself back to the apartment block, garaged the Fiesta, went into the flat and deposited her bag . . . and then for some reason left again. In such a hurry that she left her bag and keys behind. Isn't that going to give rise to an awful lot of speculation?'

'Of course it is.'

'All right. You're counting on it confusing the issue, to such an extent—'

Striding towards her, Simon took up a position alongside her with an elbow on the worktop. Their faces were a foot apart. A streak of dirt, she noticed, darkened the skin under his right eye. She felt an urge to wash it off. At the same time, she didn't want to touch him.

His voice was almost expressionless. 'As long as they can't find a body, how are they going to pin anything on anyone?'

For a long moment her eyes challenged his. 'Won't it be found, though? Can you be certain?'

'In my considered judgement,' Simon said in a scholarly manner which at any other time she would have found ludicrous, 'the chances of that happening are so negligible as to be not worth considering. Okay? Satisfied?'

'Where have you hidden her?'

'I'm not going to tell you.'

'I have to know.'

'It's better that you don't.'

Jo chewed her lip. 'You think I might tell someone?'

'Things can slip out. As long as you genuinely have no idea, you can't . . . make a mistake. Can you?'

'But you can.'

He shrugged. 'It's a matter of cutting down the risk to the minimum. Once start sharing a secret, you might as well go ahead and broadcast it on all channels every night of the week. It's as simple as that.'

Jo stared across the kitchen. 'I've no wish to know,' she said slowly. 'All I want to do is forget the whole ghastly business.'

Giving her arm a quick pat, Simon went away to the sink. 'That's the spirit.' Extracting the pink rubber hand-protectors from his zip pocket, he hung them back on their hook, stood off to contemplate them. 'The right approach, entirely. It never happened. Erase it. All that counts is that we're together again—you, me and Carol. Nothing else matters. Now let's go to bed.'

CHAPTER 12

To Nigel Fielding, assistant manager of the Southweald branch of Granger's Sterling Foodmarket, the unheralded descent from Head Office of a pair of high-powered middle executives represented a golden chance for him to make an impression. A young man of ambition, Nigel was invariably at his post by eight-twenty, a feat which so far had cut little ice with anybody, least of all his immediate superior, who was himself inclined to take punctuality to excess. This morning, however, Nigel had managed to arrive first, just in time to admit the two high-powered executives as they arrived in their Vauxhall Carlton. And it was still twelve minutes to opening time. He hoped the point had been noted.

The executives, lean and streamlined, close-packed with ideas, got straight down to work. 'Better use,' pronounced one, 'could be made of *that* area, for starters. Those racks could swing round. Ease congestion at the checkouts.'

'Or they could be doubled up,' Nigel suggested boldly. 'Take them back a yard, allow more trolley space.'

Neither executive betrayed any sign of having heard him. Drawing breath to try again, Nigel saw with dejection that Simon was approaching from the street, having left his car in its usual place in the loading yard at the rear of the building. Punctual to the minute, as usual. Or rather, ten minutes early, as always. Was the man ever to show a chink in his armour? Resigned to yet another tactical defeat, Nigel opened the glass door to admit him and introduced the visitors from Head Office, who, he was secretly gratified to observe, took little more notice of the manager than they had of his deputy as they remained in postures of contemplation, assessing square footage and display angles. Not that this seemed to affect Simon. Alert as ever, he took over the role of station commander from Nigel, who melted away discreetly to their small, shared office beyond the food shelves and launched himself upon the morning's administrative workload, hatching plans at the back of his mind for better exploitation of a visit from the top brass if the opportunity should recur.

Half an hour later Simon joined him. 'I've left them measuring up,' he reported, 'in Canned Soups. They seem to think it could be merged with Bread and Biscuits. I doubt if they'll be here more than another twenty minutes. Apparently they're going on to Hove.'

'Full of ideas, aren't they?'

'That's what they're paid to be.'

'Reverting to things that matter,' Nigel said whimsically, 'do you know whether Polly's coming in this morning?'

'Polly Gathercole? I assume so. Why, hasn't she turned up?'

'Not yet. She's normally here well before nine.'

Simon consulted his watch. 'Car trouble, perhaps. She'll be along. If she was ill, she'd have phoned in by now.'

'Shall I give her a call?'

'Would you mind, Nigel? If there's no answer, she's

probably on her way.' Seating himself at his desk, Simon examined the day's stock report.

'No reply,' said his assistant, moments later. 'Looks like you were right—she's mending a puncture or stuck in a traffic jam. I'll go and tell Jackie to stand in for her till she arrives.'

As Nigel strode from the office, the visiting executives marched in. 'We'll be off, then, Mr Pettigrew,' announced the taller and thinner of the pair. 'We think we've—'

'Pettifer.'

'Sorry. Confusing you with someone at Hove branch.' Why, the executive wondered to himself, were managerial staff so touchy about names? What did it matter? 'As I say, we think we've identified one or two sectors of spatial revision and you'll be getting some people down shortly to implement them. Otherwise it all seems to be ticking over. No staff problems?'

'They're a good bunch. One latecomer this morning, but that's not typical.'

'Who is it?'

'Our checkout supervisor, Miss Gathercole. We think she's probably hit traffic trouble on her way in.'

'Normally quite reliable, eh? We believe you, my boy,' the executive said jovially.

'Would you care for a coffee?'

'No time, thanks. Three more visits to make today. So long.'

In the wake of their departure, Simon paid a visit to the checkouts. Jackie Sinclair, a pinched-faced young woman who took things seriously, was looking anxious. 'No sign of her yet, Mr Pettifer.'

'Who's that, Jackie?'

'Polly Gathercole,' she said reproachfully. Who did he think she meant? 'Only we've got problems on the Cash Only till. Celia's on it, that new girl, and she's done something, I don't know what it is, but she's pressed something she shouldn't have and it's gone on the blink and she's going into hysterics and we—'

'Open up another till,' Simon advised. 'Transfer the customers, then call Frank. I'll have another shot at contacting Polly.'

A muted gonging sound came from the public address system. 'Call for Mr Pettifer. Telephone call, please, Mr Pettifer.'

'That might be her now,' he remarked. Fighting his way back through predatory shoppers to the office, he picked up his receiver. 'Simon Pettifer here.'

'Is this the manager's extension?'

'Manager speaking. Can I help?'

'I'm wanting to speak to Miss Gathercole. They put me through to you.'

'I'm afraid she's not here just now. Can I ask her to ring you?'

'Can't you fetch her to the phone?'

The voice was male, unceremonious. Simon said, 'She hasn't arrived yet. We're expecting her at any minute. Who's calling?'

'Not in? I thought she had to be there by eight-thirty.'

'Evidently she's been delayed. Who—'

'I've tried her flat twice already,' complained the caller. 'If she's not there and she's not with you, where the bloody hell is she? I'm her brother and she was supposed to call me.'

'The moment she shows up, I'll get her to give you a buzz.'

'Tell her it's Clive, will you?'

'I'll do that, Mr Gathercole.'

There was a short pause. 'Did you say your name was Simon?'

'Simon Pettifer, that's right. Why do you ask?'

'No reason. Be grateful, then, if you'll pass on the message. Cheers.'

'Cheers.' Simon put the receiver down.

At midday Nigel Fielding conducted a uniformed policeman into the office. 'Constable Hall to see you, Simon.'

'Hullo, Constable. What's it about? Another shoplifting epidemic?'

'He's inquiring about Polly Gathercole,' Nigel said informatively.

Simon came to his feet. 'She's not been in an accident?'

'This is what we're trying to establish, sir.' Police Constable Hall, a kindly disposed thirty-year-old, disliked any premature allusion to possible catastrophe. 'I've just been having a word with her brother, Mr Clive Gathercole, who apparently was expecting to hear from her first thing this morning . . .'

'He phoned here, earlier.'

'Seems to be flapping a bit. But then he may have cause. I understand from Mr Fielding here that Miss Gathercole doesn't make a habit of staying away without notifying you?'

'She never has, up to now. Have you been round to her apartment?'

Hall nodded. 'No answer to the doorbell, so with her brother's permission I forced an entry. She wasn't there.'

'No sign of a disturbance?'

'Everything in apple-pie order. Just one slightly puzzling thing . . .'

'What was that, Constable?'

'Her handbag. It had been left on a chair in the lounge.'

'Maybe she didn't want to be lumbered with it.'

'But all her keys were inside. Flat, garage, car.'

Simon sat on his desk. 'That's certainly odd. Unless she has duplicates to them all. In which case, where would she keep them? You're absolutely positive she's not somewhere inside the apartment?'

'We made a thorough search of the premises,' Hall said with dignified restraint.

'In that case I don't understand it. When she left us last night, she seemed fine. Full of bounce.'

'When she left here, you mean?'

'No. I'm talking about when she drove away from my house.' Simon glanced up. 'Sorry—you weren't aware of that, of course. My wife and I had her over last evening, for coffee. She took off for home about . . . oh, between ten-thirty and eleven. Somewhere around then. At that time there was definitely no hint of anything wrong.'

'Miss Gathercole, then—' Constable Hall coughed—'was a personal friend of yours, then, as well as an employee?'

Nigel looked at his superior in some surprise. He had not been aware that Polly was on more than formal terms with the manager. Another spasm darted through his chest. Whichever way he turned, Simon seemed to be three steps ahead of him. It was disheartening.

'Actually,' Simon was explaining, 'it's my wife she's more acquainted with. They got to know each other some while back, when they both patronized the same hairdresser. That's how Polly landed the job here, in fact. My wife tipped her off about the vacancy.'

A glint of humour shone from the constable's eyes. 'The Old Girl Network,' he murmured. 'It's one way of licking unemployment. So, Miss Gathercole left your place last night, sir, an hour or so before midnight? In good form? No suggestion of . . . illness?'

'She wasn't tight, if that's what you're asking. She'd drunk nothing.'

'Except coffee, I take it.'

'A cup and a half of black coffee and two biscuits. Those dry cracker things. She has a slight weight problem. If she was feeling unwell when she left,' Simon added thoughtfully, 'she hid it like a trouper, that's all I can say.'

'Might she have mentioned anything to your wife?'

'It's possible. You could ask her.'

'We may do that. Although, on the other hand,' Hall said after a brief pause, 'the fact that Miss Gathercole's car is back inside her garage seems to confirm that she was well enough to drive herself home. Unless the sickness came on later . . . early morning, say.'

'But if so, why would she leave the flat?'

'Maybe she wanted to be first at the doctor's surgery,' suggested Nigel.

'In that case, she'd have taken her bag and keys. But in any case, the surgery wouldn't have been open at that hour.'

'What hour?' Nigel demanded smartly.

Simon gestured. 'Crack of dawn, presumably. Otherwise she'd have been spotted by someone. It's hard to be invisible in an urban district from seven o'clock onwards.'

'Besides,' Constable Hall interjected, 'the surgery has no record of her calling in this morning.'

'What if she'd cut herself badly, with a kitchen knife or something? She might have gone running straight to the nearest casualty department.'

Hall shook his head. 'That's been checked. No hospital in the area has treated anyone of that name, or anyone like her.'

Simon gave Nigel a helpless look. 'You think we should leave it a few more hours, in case she shows up?'

'Quite frankly, sir,' replied Hall, taking the question as having been directed at himself, 'I don't see that we've much option. She can't be conjured out of nowhere.'

'No, but surely the search could be stepped up, on the offchance that . . .' Simon stopped, rubbed his neck. 'Forgive me, Constable. I didn't mean to sound bossy. You know your job a lot better than I do.'

'That's quite all right, sir.'

'It's just that one can't help feeling a bit agitated. It's so out of character for Polly to do anything of this sort. Could she possibly . . .'

'Possibly what?'

'I was wondering if she might have suffered a sudden loss of memory. You do read of such things.'

'It happens,' Hall said non-committally. 'Has she been under stress lately, would you know?'

'I'm afraid I wouldn't.'

'We'll ask her brother. Meanwhile, sir, if she does happen to breeze back in here, you will let us know immediately? Save a lot of wasted effort.'

At two-fifteen, when Simon was at lunch, a second call came through from Clive Gathercole. It was dealt with by Nigel Fielding.

'The bloke sounded really uptight,' he reported on Simon's return. 'Seemed to think there was something more definite we could do about Polly. I told him the cops were handling it. He said he knew that, but why weren't we making more inquiries ourselves? What sort of inquiries, I asked him. He was a bit vague about that, but when I—'

'He's worried about his sister,' Simon said on a key of tolerance. 'Only natural. We'll have to expect a bit of wild talk, until she shows up.'

Clive's third call came through at four, and was taken by Simon. 'I've been talking to the police,' Polly's brother declared without ceremony, 'and they tell me my sister was up at your place last night.'

'So she was, Mr Gathercole. We had coffee and a chat. She left some time before eleven.'

'What was the chat about?'

'I beg your pardon?'

'What was it *about*? You must have had something to discuss.'

'Ever hear of a social occasion?' Simon inquired. 'It was along the lines of one of those.'

'I've heard of social occasions. We were planning one, Polly and me. A foursome, tomorrow night. She was going to invite someone from your Frozen Foods department . . . Irene?'

'Irene Mablethorpe. They're quite good friends, I believe.'

'Whether she got around to it, I don't know. She was going to tell me when she rang this morning. I'm not clear who the other guy was going to be, either. Do you have any idea?'

'Why should I?'

'She was talking about some bloke called Simon.'

'Was she?'

'That's your first name, isn't it?'

'Yes. But I'm not the one she was referring to, if that's what you're suggesting. I happen to be married.'

'She did go and see you last night.'

'My wife and me. It was a long-standing invitation.'

'Funny.'

'What do you mean?'

'The impression I got was exactly the opposite. The way she told it to me, she was looking in on the pair of you whether you liked it or not.'

'I don't quite understand.'

'She said she'd something to thrash out with you.'

'As far as I'm aware,' Simon said on a reflective note, 'your sister, Mr Gathercole, had no cause for complaint on any aspect of her terms of employment here at Granger's. She certainly never—'

'I'm not talking about Granger's.'

'Just what are you talking about, then?'

There was a short interval. 'I'll leave you,' said Clive, 'to think that one over, Mr Pettifer.' He hung up.

Nigel glanced across. 'Our friend starting to get obstreperous?'

'Working himself into something of a lather,' Simon replied absently. Presently he rose, walked outside and headed for Frozen Foods. Two besmocked young women were replenishing the freezers from tall trolleys. One of them, a straw-blonde with buck teeth, looked up at his approach.

'Any word from Polly, Mr Pettifer?'

'Not yet, Irene. Tell me something. Did she make any kind of arrangement with you yesterday? For an outing?'

'She did ask me if I fancied a foursome tomorrow night. Her and her brother. He's here from up North for a few days.' Irene offered a facial grimace suggestive of regret. 'Only I had to say no, on account of it's me mum's birthday and she'd kill me if I toddled off for the evening. I dunno if Polly got anyone else. Why?'

'Her brother just mentioned it to me.' Simon leaned over to realign the display of fresh cream gateaux. 'It's probably not important. I just thought it might possibly explain her non-appearance today. Unlikely, though. Not like her at all.'

'Polly always puts her work first,' Irene said primly.

'Of course she does. I know that. Don't worry about it, Irene. There's sure to be a simple explanation. She'll be back at her post tomorrow, no question.'

'Let's hope so, Mr Pettifer.' Irene gazed a little vacantly at the frozen Black Forest gateau she was clasping between her mittened hands. 'Otherwise they'll really have to start looking, won't they?'

CHAPTER 13

Hearing the grinding of tyres on the gravel, Jo hurried out to the porch.

Simon, she thought with relief, had managed to get away early. Her desire to talk to him had built up steadily throughout the day and was now at bursting point. Only the emphasis of his instructions, as he left that morning, had held her back from telephoning him at Granger's.

The car standing outside was not the Renault. It was a

stripe-marked Montego with a POLICE sign on the roof. The sight of it nearly rocked her back into the hall. Forcing herself to stand her ground, she waited while the car disgorged its occupant, a stocky figure in sergeant's uniform who stood appraising the house for a moment before scrunching towards her at a stately pace. She remembered to keep some modest apprehension in her expression. It was not too difficult.

'What is it?' she called. 'Don't tell me my husband's run the car into a tree?'

Smilingly the sergeant shook his head, joined her in the porch. 'No problem, Mrs Pettifer, far as you're concerned. Well, I say there's no problem—you may feel different about it. Depends how good a friend you are—' he eyed her warily —'of Miss Gathercole.'

'Polly? Why, Sergeant? Has something happened to her?'

'That,' he said solemnly, 'she's not here to tell us, more's the pity. Seems she's taken herself off.'

'Taken off?'

'Without so much as leaving a forwarding address. The reason I'm here, Mrs Pettifer . . . it's understood you had a visit from her last night?'

'That's right. She came for coffee. Taken off?' Jo repeated on a note of perplexity. 'Why would she do such a thing?'

'Now that's asking. She never reported for work this morning and she never phoned in.' Briefly the sergeant explained the circumstances. 'So we're asking around, like,' he concluded. 'Hoping you might be able to help. Seeing as you and your husband must've been just about the last to clap eyes on her.'

Jo leaned attentively against the sill of the porch window. 'What is it you'd like to know?'

'Well, for openers . . . Miss Gathercole would've been with you for how long?'

'Let's see. She arrived about eight-thirty and she left . . .

somewhere around a quarter to eleven. As far as we knew, she was intending to drive straight back to her flat in Southweald. Didn't she?'

'Her car's there, tucked away in the garage. Not a sign of her, though.'

'How extraordinary. If the car had been missing, I might have understood it.'

'How's that, Mrs Pettifer?'

'Polly's a bit on the impulsive side. I wouldn't have put it past her to suddenly hit on the idea of driving off to visit someone else—a relative or someone,' Jo said with a hint of reticence, 'and perhaps lose track of the time a little. I'm sure she'd be capable of it.'

The sergeant looked nonplussed. 'Lose track of a night and a day?'

'It might depend,' Jo said coyly, 'on just who she was visiting.'

His face cleared. 'I believe I follow. Still, though, that doesn't account for the car, does it? You'd think she'd have used it to go wherever she was going. Unless it was nearby. And if it was nearby, why hasn't she been in touch?'

'It's certainly baffling.' Jo glanced up at him. 'Did you want to come inside, Sergeant? Very rude of me, keeping you here on the step.'

'Not a bit of it. Tell you what, though. It might help if I could take a quick look where Miss Gathercole was sitting last night. Never know what you might find.'

'I didn't notice anything when I tidied up this morning, but you're welcome to see for yourself.' Leading him through to the living-room, Jo pointed to the relevant armchair. 'That's where she sat—the entire evening, as far as I recall. She had coffee and dry biscuits.'

'That all?'

'She doesn't touch alcohol. She's trying to slim.'

'Take anything, does she, for that?'

'Pills, you mean? I've no idea. She might.'

'Only if she did, and she was to overdo it . . .'

'I see what you mean,' she breathed.

The sergeant moved closer to the armchair. 'You've swept, I dare say, around the furniture this morning?'

'Hoovered, actually.'

'So,' he mused, 'if Miss Gathercole *did* chance to be on tablets, and she *were* to have popped a few with her coffee last night, and one or two of 'em *had* accidentally found their way on to the carpet . . . odds are, they'd be inside your cleaner bag?'

'I suppose so. Want to take a look? It's in the hall cupboard.'

Spilling the appliance's matted contents on to an old copy of the Southweald *Beacon*, the sergeant devoted ten minutes to a heavy-breathing perusal of the heap, sifting cautiously with meaty fingertips. Eventually he rose with a gasp and a sigh. 'No clues in that lot, sad to say. Not to the naked eye, that is. Mind if I take it away, Mrs Pettifer? You wouldn't happen to have a plastic bag handy?'

She found him one in a kitchen drawer. Thanking her gravely, he inserted the bundled copy of the *Beacon* with scrupulous care and sealed the neck of the bag. 'Most grateful for your time,' he informed her, trudging towards the front door. 'Should you remember anything else, or hear from Miss Gathercole . . .' He came to a halt. 'One thing I was meaning to ask. We've spoken to your husband, but would there be any other member of your family who might be in a position to assist?'

'There's my small daughter, Carol. But she was upstairs in bed the whole time Polly was here.'

'In that case I'll be getting along. Sorry to be a nuisance.'

'It's no bother. I do hope you've some news soon.'

'Did he seem satisfied?'

'I think so. He took the bag of dirt from the cleaner, which I assume they'll analyse or something.' Jo hesitated, spoke again with an effort. 'They're . . . not likely to find anything? I mean, there was no . . .'

'It was just a smack of the head,' Simon said brusquely, 'against the wall. The skin wasn't broken. Did he say anything about coming back? Holding ourselves available?'

'Nothing like that.'

Splashing soda into his whisky glass, Simon took a regardless gulp while staring across the garden. The sun, making a comeback during the day, had carried the shade temperature once more up into the seventies Fahrenheit and was now carrying out an evening inspection of the tops of the Downs. Jo had changed into a thinner frock. Before doing so, she had taken another hot bath. Her third that day. She couldn't seem to get herself clean.

Simon looked heavily preoccupied. The information about the sergeant's inquiries had made little obvious impression on him. Casting him one or two uncertain glances, Jo drank down her dry martini, sat looking at the glass, took the plunge.

'Would you think anybody suspects?'

'Why should they?'

'Any number of reasons. She was here, after all, just a few hours before . . .' Jo struggled with the order of her thoughts. 'Then again, it might seem fishy to a lot of people, her being here at all.'

'Why?'

'Nobody knew her as a friend of mine.'

'They do now.'

'You think they'll all be convinced?'

'If anyone wants to question it,' said Simon, swallowing more Scotch, 'that's entirely up to them.'

She sat watching the sunlight on the Downs.

'You're quite certain nobody knew there was a relationship between you?'

Simon's garden chair scraped the terrace flagstones as he changed position. 'We kept it completely under wraps.

Neither of us wanted it bandied around. In the store, we were boss and employee—nothing else.'

'People can get to know.'

'I can't imagine how. Anyway, so what? They can't prove anything.'

From one hilltop, hang-gliders were taking off, wheeling and swooping on the thermal currents. Seen from beneath, they were giant dragonflies lazily buzzing the landscape. Already, seven were airborne. Others were assembling for launch.

'They might. If they found her.'

The whisky glass quivered a little. 'They won't.'

'How can you be so positive?'

'Because I was thorough.'

'Tell me what you did.'

From inside the living-room, orchestral music swelled to engulf the terrace. Simon turned his head to glance into the dim interior. 'That child ought to be out here enjoying the sunshine, not glued to the box. No wonder she gets pale.'

'You haven't answered my question.'

'Because I don't intend to. The subject's closed.'

'Is it somewhere that—'

'I've made my position clear, Jo. Don't push me.'

Rising, he went indoors. Jo sat on, superficially aware of the hang-gliders' gyrations against the green and blue backdrop of slope and sky. One outrider hovered almost vertically overhead. From where she sat he was plainly visible, strapped to his featherweight harness, face down, scanning their garden like a housewife looking for dust. Intrusion of privacy. If they liked, she wondered vaguely, would householders be justified in shooting him out of their airspace?

Re-emerging with the whisky bottle, Simon fortified his glass. 'Carol seems quiet. You've not been getting at her?'

'Me? Why should I?'

'We mustn't ask her any questions about what she saw or heard.'

'I hope I've more sense.'

'We have to keep our cool. Then she'll do the same. If she asks outright, our friend Polly came for the evening and we had a noisy discussion about politics which woke her up. That's it. She mustn't be given the chance to start embroidering.'

'Carol's not in the habit of telling stories.'

'Children can imagine things,' he insisted. 'Especially if they're woken out of sleep. They can get things twisted.'

'Or straight.'

He flung her a glance. 'As long as we keep our heads,' he reiterated after an interval, 'we should have nothing to worry about. From any quarter.'

They sat observing the sky-riders. Presently Jo said apathetically, 'Are you ready for your meal?'

'It can wait. Did you speak to your mother today?'

'She phoned, lunch-time.'

'To ask after progress?'

'Progress?'

'The extension,' Simon said testily. 'She must wonder what's going on.'

'She knows there's bound to be some delay. I didn't actually tell her it's going to be longer than we thought. Should I?'

'No, don't. I spoke to Fenshaw today.'

'Who's Fenshaw?'

'Building contractor in Hove. Did a job for us at the back of the store last year. Obliging sort of guy. Says he'd be willing to take over the annexe from Hawkins.'

Jo sat up. 'When could he make a start?'

'Right away.'

'And you believe him?'

'I've no reason not to. He was spot on with the Granger's project. Turned up with his gang on the agreed date, got on with it, did a first-rate job in the time allotted. Top-class bloke.'

'If he's that sensational, what made you choose—' Jo paused fleetingly—'someone else for our scheme?'

'Fenshaw charges more. And he has further to come, of course. But in the circumstances, as things have panned out . . .'

'All right, get Fenshaw along. Can we afford him?'

'We'll have to.'

Jo turned her head to study him. 'I thought we were already operating at the limit?'

'Taking the long-term view,' Simon said authoritatively, 'it should turn out to be an investment. Anyhow, your mother's anxious to come here and you're keen to have her—right? No sense in putting it off. Building costs are going to rocket, whatever happens.'

Jo stared down the garden. 'Can Fenshaw work from the existing plans?'

'He says so. And Hawkins has agreed to pass them over.'

'How do you know?'

'I contacted him as well.'

'You have been active.' The faint acidity in her voice surprised herself, but Simon appeared not to notice, or at least to place no weight upon her reaction. He sent another glance across his shoulder into the room.

'It'll be nice for Carol.'

'Having her Nan here?'

Simon nodded. 'Better all round, in fact. Give you something to think about in the meantime, besides. Take your mind off things.'

The telephone shrilled as Simon was eating his supper. When she answered, Jo's eardrum was afflicted by a male voice of such resonance that she held the receiver away, wincing.

'Mrs Pettifer? Sorry to bother you at this hour. Chief

Inspector Walter Dean here, Southweald CID. I was wondering if it might be possible to have a quick word with your husband? Is he available?'

Her heart bounced painfully. 'He's . . . just in the middle of a meal.'

'In that case, perhaps he wouldn't mind calling me back? The number to ring—'

'Just a second. He's here.'

At her elbow, Simon took over the instrument. 'Simon Pettifer. Who? Oh yes, Chief Inspector. Yes, your Constable Hall did speak to me earlier on today, and I believe he mentioned your name. It's about Miss Gathercole, I expect. Any news?'

While he listened, Jo dithered at the living-room door. Simon was looking at her, seeing something else.

'A work problem? No, I think I can scotch that one. She was right on top of her job. And got on well with the rest of the staff. Private worries? Well of course, that's a different kettle of fish . . .'

He listened again. 'Now that you ask, there is something I'd noticed during the past few weeks. Not depression, exactly—at least that's not how it struck me. But then I don't pretend to . . . Well, she did seem to have this tendency now and then to let her mind wander. Not when she was working, no. Off-guard moments. But I must emphasize, it was just a vague impression on my part . . .'

Listening once more, he assumed a slight frown. 'Not while she was here, no—certainly not. She seemed positively bursting with high spirits. We got on to politics, and things became so animated our little girl was woken up by the noise—from two floors above! It was all great fun. Which is why it came as such a shock today, hearing she'd gone missing . . .'

Walking past him to the stairs, Jo mounted to the first landing and stood there for a moment, cupping her ear. No sound came from the attic. Carol, looking sleepy, had gone to bed before Simon started his supper: the sleeping pill, Jo thought, might still be having a residual effect.

'Quite true,' Simon was saying as she descended to the hall. 'Only a matter of twenty-four hours, isn't it? If she's missing a second night, things might start to look more . . . Yes, be glad to. I'm home by seven, normally. Your sergeant did take a look this afternoon, my wife tells me. All right, Chief Inspector. Tomorrow evening, around eight. Thanks for calling. 'Night.'

Replacing the receiver, Simon stood with a hand upon it. 'An official visit,' he said slowly, 'from the detective in charge of the case. Inevitable, I suppose. We might as well face up to it. Just bear in mind what I said.'

'Eight o'clock,' Jo said shakily. 'That's late enough to give us an excuse to pack Carol off to bed again. She'll—'

Simon shook his head. 'He wants to speak to her as well.'

CHAPTER 14

The heat of the classroom was making the desk lids sticky. When Carol tried to remove her bare forearms from the support of the varnished woodwork, it clung to her skin before falling back with a thump that stopped Miss Harris, the geography teacher, in her tracks as she tried to explain rainfall patterns in Southern England. Displeased, she called Carol a little troublemaker. The injustice of it hurt Carol but she took it on the chin, exchanging rueful looks with Lynda and reminding herself that it didn't matter, nothing mattered as long as you knew you had nothing to be ashamed of. Another girl, Miriam Long, sent her a sympathetic smile, but Carol didn't feel up to responding. She was too hot, too drowsy. And mentally, beneath it all, too unsettled.

After school, she and Lynda were met as usual by Auntie Steph in the Metro. Auntie Steph, cool in a floral dress, conveyed an encouraging flavour of self-possession and normality. 'So what happened today, girls? Any excitement?'

'Carol got told off,' reported Lynda, 'for slamming her desktop.'

'Oh dear. Not on purpose?'

'It stuck to my hand,' Carol explained.

'Happened to me, once. Never mind. As long as *you* know it wasn't deliberate. The car's over there. I just popped into the shop for the *Beacon*. There's a bit in it, Carol, that might interest your father.'

'What?'

'Something about a member of Granger's staff going missing. He may know about it already. On the other hand, he might have been under the impression she was just absent for the day through illness. But apparently—'

'What's her name?' asked Carol. Something inside her had tightened suddenly.

'Miss Polly Gathercole,' said Auntie Steph, consulting her copy of the *Beacon*'s late edition, 'of Rowan Court, Southweald. Heard of her? She's the checkout supervisor at Granger's.'

'I think Daddy knows her.'

Auntie Steph seemed to find this amusing. 'I dare say he does, seeing they both work there. Pile in quick, both of you, I'm blocking the road. According to this, Miss Gathercole vanished after visiting friends. Her brother's very worried. He was expecting a phone call from her, yesterday morning.'

'Perhaps she'd quarrelled with him,' suggested Lynda, wriggling herself into a corner of the rear seat. 'That's why she didn't phone.'

'He says not. Anyway, a quarrel with her brother wouldn't have kept her away from her job, surely? They think she might have had some kind of nervous breakdown.'

'What's a nervous breakdown?'

'Depression, usually. It can make you do things you wouldn't normally consider.' Bouncing clear of the grass verge, Auntie Steph aimed the car at the bend. 'Overwork can cause it. Worry. Anything like that. Once you get really down in the mouth, it can be quite hard to . . .'

Half-hearing the dialogue, Carol sat staring out at the shifting contours of the Downs as the Metro pursued the series of eight curves that led to her parents' house. At the gateway she scrambled out hurriedly. 'Thank you, Auntie Steph. Bye-bye, Lynda.'

'See you in the morning, dear. Usual time. Tell your mother I'll be in touch. And tell your father—'

Stephanie's voice trailed off. No reply had come from Carol, who was already several yards away up the drive. 'She's in a hurry,' she remarked to Lynda, swinging the Metro round to head for home. 'Were you given a lot of homework to get through?'

'We weren't given any.'

'Not like her to rush off like that.' Stephanie felt vaguely troubled as she drove off.

At Carol's entry, her mother advanced down the hall with an unnaturally wide smile to greet her. 'Hi, darling. Make out all right at school?'

'Yes, thank you.' Carol stood motionless to receive a kiss on the cheek.

'I've scrambled you an egg.'

'I'm not very hungry.'

'Eat what you can. There won't be time later. We're having another visitor.'

Carol's stomach gave a lurch. 'Who?'

'Just someone from the police station in Southweald. He won't be staying long. Just wants to ask us all a few questions.'

'What about?'

Producing a hairbrush from her smock pocket, her mother moved in behind her. 'Remember the lady from Daddy's store who called the night before last? Apparently she—'

'I know. Auntie Steph told me.'

The hairbrush loitered on her scalp. 'About Miss Gathercole disappearing? How did she hear of it?'

'She read it in the *Beacon*.'

'Oh.' The hairbrush resumed its scratchy caress. 'Well, the point is, as she'd been with us the previous evening—Miss Gathercole, I mean—the police want to ask us whether we can give them any clues as to where she might have gone. That's all. It shouldn't take long.'

'Will you be able to?'

'Offer any clues? Hardly. All we can tell them is what sort of mood she was in while she was here. High-spirited, about sums it up. You saw her, didn't you, darling, for a moment? She was quite bouncy, wouldn't you say?'

Carol was silent.

Again the hairbrush came to a stop. 'If the policeman asks, you must give him a reply. What will you say?'

Carol's voice was faint. 'She did sound a bit excited . . .'

'That's a good word. Excited—yes. That describes it rather nicely. Remember to tell him that.'

'Supposing he asks me something else?'

'If you're uncertain about anything, just say you don't know. You didn't see much of her, did you? Barely more than a glimpse. And you were half-asleep.'

'What time is he coming?' Carol slid clear of the nylon bristles to remove her blazer. She felt muzzy-headed, stickier than ever. And she genuinely had no appetite.

'The policeman? Not long after Daddy gets home, I should think. You can look in at the ice-skating till he arrives.'

The policeman, to Carol's bafflement but slight relief, was clad not in uniform but in casual jacket and slacks, much less formal than her father's working attire. On the other hand, he was accompanied by a lady policeman rigged out in the full gear of regulation blouse and skirt, although her peaked cap, if she had one, had evidently been left in the car. Carol assumed there was a car. Few people called on them unless they had one. The policeman, who had a kindly, chubby face and was rather smaller than she had anticipated, stooped to shake her hand with some solemnity.

'Good evening, Carol. Ever been asked to help the police with their inquiries before?'

'No.' Overawed though she felt, she was determined not to show it. Unluckily she was overtaken by a sudden shortage of breath, so that her voice emerged as a faint quaver. He didn't seem to mind.

'So now you'll be able to tell your chums how we operate. Know what I am? I'm a chief inspector. That over there is WPC Caroline Grant. Same first name as yours, only more of it. Know what we're here about?'

Carol nodded. 'Miss Gathercole.'

'That's it. The lady who's done a vanishing trick on us. You saw her, I'm told, a couple of nights back. I've just been asking your parents about her. Now it's your turn. Ready?'

'Answer the Chief Inspector clearly, Carol.' The instruction came from her father, who was standing in a relaxed position by the dresser. Her mother was seated in her usual armchair, quite still, straight-backed, grave and attentive.

'She'll do her level best, I know. First of all, then, Carol—what time of the evening was it when you saw Miss Gathercole? Can you tell me that?'

Carol glanced at her mother, who looked back at her but said nothing. 'I think it was about . . . I don't know exactly. I'd been asleep.'

'Do you have a wristwatch?'

Carol shook her head. 'There's a clock on my bedside locker.'

'Did you look at it at all?'

She screwed up her eyes. 'I did when I went back upstairs.'

'And what did it say?'

'I think it said ten o'clock.'

'All right. Fine. Let's say you saw Miss Gathercole a few minutes before that. Now, how did she strike you? I mean, was she cheerful or was she miserable?'

'I don't think she was miserable . . .'

Carol's hesitation became a full stop. She couldn't think how to continue. Having waited, the chief inspector said supportively, 'Hard to tell with a person sometimes, I know. When you came into the room, was she talking?'

'Yes.'

'What was she saying, can you recall?'

'Not really . . .'

'Was it about herself?'

Carol gazed at him dumbly.

Her mother made a slight movement. 'Perhaps it's asking rather a lot to expect—'

'I *do* ask a lot,' the chief inspector agreed readily. 'I'm allowing for that. And I don't want to put words into Carol's mouth. If you honestly can't recollect any more, Carol, I'd like you to say so, here and now. One more question. When you came in, did Miss Gathercole notice you?'

'Yes. She spoke to me.'

'Ah. Remember anything she said?'

From the corner of an eye, Carol could see her parents watching her intently. Their expressions told her nothing. Her mind filmed over. She discovered that, without having consciously engineered it, she was shaking her head again. But that was wrong. There were one or two things she did remember. On the brink of mentioning them, she was forestalled by the chief inspector, who was looking chubbier by the minute.

'No. Well, we won't take it further than that. Thank you, Carol. You've been jolly helpful and we appreciate it. Now I expect there's a TV programme you want to see . . . or is it homework first? Get much homework, do you?'

'A token amount,' put in her father, smiling at her. 'When

you go on from the primary—that's when you'll know all about it, eh poppet?'

An answering smile seemed to be expected of her, so Carol obliged. Her mother, she couldn't help noticing, didn't smile. She was observing the lady policeman, who for her part was directing a fairly close scrutiny at Carol herself, as if trying to make out whether she had washed her neck recently. Carol felt acute discomfort. She wished the two of them would go. The chief inspector, however, had a thing or two more to say.

'If Miss Gathercole should make contact with you or anyone else at the store, you'll notify us immediately, Mr Pettifer?'

'Of course.'

'Likewise, if any of your staff has an inspiration. You know. Something Miss Gathercole might have mentioned lately; something she might have done. The smallest thing out of the ordinary. It just might provide a lead.'

'Understood. I've been racking my own brains, but . . .' Carol's father made a regretful gesture. 'You've not happened upon anything yourself, Mr Dean?'

'What we've mainly encountered,' replied the chief inspector lugubriously, 'is the *lack* of anything exceptional. I mean as regards her personal circumstances. There's her flat, all neat and tidy, bed not slept in, not a trace of disturbance in sight. There's her car, tucked away inside her garage, fuel tank half full, handbrake applied, steering lock engaged. She didn't leave it in any hurry, that's for sure. On the contrary. More care seemed to have been taken with it than your average motorist would bother about, considering it was being left behind a steel door.' Dean beamed at Carol's father. 'Characteristic, would you say? Fairly scrupulous kind of person, is she, in her job?'

'Attentive to detail,' Simon returned promptly. 'She needs to be, of course. When you're dealing with computerized tills and customer manœuvres, life can get pretty hectic at times.'

'Glad I leave the shopping to my wife.' Dean turned the beam upon his female subordinate for an instant before switching it back. 'What you're saying is, then, Miss Gathercole's hardly the type to lose her head in a crisis?'

'I wouldn't have thought so. Not a business crisis.'

'An emotional one?'

'I dare say most of us are more susceptible to those.'

'You never spoke a truer word,' the chief inspector announced heartily. 'Still, even if we assume for the sake of argument that Miss Gathercole received some sudden shattering news when she arrived home the night before last —news which sent her dashing out again before she'd had a chance to sit down—it leaves a hell of a lot unexplained. Why hasn't she contacted anyone since? Why didn't she take her bag?'

'Because,' suggested Jo, 'she was caught completely off balance.'

Chief Inspector Dean eyed the ceiling. 'Does that figure? I suppose it might.'

'Not in my experience, sir.' The intervention came from WPC Grant, who removed her gaze from Carol while she was talking, to the child's thankfulness. 'If anyone had put it to me, I'd have said it was practically unheard of for any woman to hurry out of her home without making a grab for her bag—or a purse, at least. However distraught she was. More especially if she'd only just come in, and the bag was staring at her from a chair.'

'There's bound to be the exception,' murmured Jo.

'I'd be inclined,' said Simon, 'to keep an open mind about it. You've forgotten your purse and keys, haven't you, dear, on occasion? Not many people are entirely immune to lapses of concentration. Polly's never struck me as one to let her mind wander, but maybe there's always a first time.'

With his gaze now aimed at the carpet, the chief inspector

went into deep reflection. Returning smoothly to his surroundings after a while, he made a sign to his junior colleague.

'We'll be getting along. See what tomorrow brings. Charming, peaceful place you've got here, Mr Pettifer. A real haven. Tiny bit isolated at times, perhaps? But you probably picked on it for that very reason. On a summer evening like this . . . perfect. No need to see us out, Mrs Pettifer, thanks awfully. We'll find our way. Good night, Carol. Thanks again.'

She gave them a timid wave as they left the room. Despite what the chief inspector had said, her mother followed them into the hall and there was another barely audible exchange of remarks before the eventual opening of the porch door. Carol sent her father a questioning look.

It seemed not to register with him. He was staring out at the garden. She released a nervous cough. Her father blinked, smiled across.

'Well done, treasure. Enjoy your first brush with the law?'

Not knowing what he meant, Carol skirted the question. 'Why did that lady policeman look at me all the time?'

'Did she? I didn't notice. What did you think of the chief inspector?'

'He didn't seem very clever.'

'You can't always judge by appearances.' The abstracted look had re-entered her father's eyes. Distantly, the porch door clumped shut. After a moment her mother came back. Carol saw a quick look pass between her parents. Her father said, 'End of inquisition. For the night.'

He was talking in riddles. Offering no reply, her mother walked quickly across to the television and, almost at random, jabbed a programme on to the screen. An American thriller: Carol identified the series with a practised eye. Normally she wasn't allowed to watch. Her father twitched an eyebrow.

'Suitable viewing for the under-sixteens?'

Her mother turned, hurried out. After a brief hesitation her father went after her.

Carol went to the living-room door. From there, she could hear their voices in the kitchen.

'Simon, I can't take much more of this. It's getting beyond me. I shan't be able to—'

'Keep your voice down. Unless you want Carol to . . .'

A sound like a sob interposed itself. Closing the door carefully, Carol tiptoed back to the sofa and picked up the TV remote control. Aiming it at the magic eye, she took the volume up to maximum.

CHAPTER 15

Doris was relieved to get the call from Jo. They hadn't spoken on the phone for four days, or was it five? She could, of course, have rung the Sussex house herself, but in the interests of prudent economy she had put it off each lunch-time, expecting Jo to take the initiative. Which she hadn't, until now.

'Sorry, Mother. I've been a bit preoccupied. Such a lot to do here, and I've been out a good deal. Also, I was waiting until we had something concrete to tell you . . . which there now is.'

'Oh?' Doris put pleased expectancy into her voice. In reality she *was* pleased and expectant, but people had told her that her reactions sometimes sounded flat, and so she had learned to over-intonate for her daughter's benefit. 'About the annexe?'

'Yes. We've decided to push ahead. This new builder—the one I mentioned before—he's agreed to make a start next Monday, so he should be arriving then.'

'How lovely. Do you think he's reliable?'

'Simon seems confident. Apparently the firm made a good

job of this coldstore they built at Granger's. So we're hoping for the best.'

'How long do they reckon it'll take?'

'The construction? Simon's talking in terms of a couple of months.'

'Good gracious. So I could be moving in by September?'

'He's probably being wildly optimistic. It must depend on the weather, any snags they might hit on. All that.'

Jo, in the opinion of her mother, sounded untypically vague; almost remote. She hoped her lively daughter wasn't starting to rusticate. Perhaps the extension project had come not a moment too soon. It might provide some fresh stimulus.

'Well, my dear, however long it takes, it'll be nice for us to be in contact again, won't it? I mean *really* in contact. How exciting. Thanks ever so much for ringing to tell me.'

'Don't bank on September. There could be a wet spell, or the builder might find he's got other—'

'Don't you worry, love. I never rely too heavily on anything. If it happens, well and good. If not, I won't lose any sleep over it.' Doris paused. 'How about yourself, Jo? You sound a bit down. Sure you *want* me over there to live?'

'Of course I do. We all do.'

'Nothing the matter with Carol?'

'No. She's fine. Everything's fine.'

On a joint shopping expedition to Southweald, in reply to Stephanie's inquiries, Jo explained briefly about the annexe.

'Yes, the builders came on Monday, as promised. In three days they've cleared the site and dug out the foundations. Quite good, they seem. I'm feeding them tea and coffee.'

'With any luck,' observed her friend, 'this fine weather may last a bit. Wouldn't it be terrific if they managed to get the shell of the building up before it rains again?'

'Probably too much to hope for.'

Stephanie eyed her companion curiously across the lunch

table in Morland's, their established rendezvous facing the pier. 'What made you ditch the first contractor? Rod Hawkins, wasn't it? Sound reputation, I thought.'

'He showed less urgency,' Jo said tersely.

On the verge of a follow-up query, Stephanie pulled back. 'I suppose,' she ventured instead, 'you *will* like having your mother close to hand?'

Jo gave the appearance of returning to the table from a distance. 'I do get bothered about her sometimes. Living alone, like she does. On the whole, we rub along quite well. And Carol's fond of her Nan.'

'I wish Lynda was the same,' Stephanie said enviously. 'She would be, I think, given the chance. But you know what my parents are like. Both on the crotchety side, now. They're happiest if we drive over to see them for half an hour, one afternoon a week.' Stephanie sighed. 'Other people have these eternally youthful, springy elder relatives whose one desire is to take over the upbringing of their grandchildren. How come I missed out?'

Expecting a comeback that would launch a debate, she was disconcerted—for the third or fourth time that morning—by the complete lack of a response. Jo appeared not even to have heard her. Gazing across the seafront at the pierhead kiosks, she was giving no attention to her prawn cocktail: eating, in fact, seemed the last thing on her mind. In the normal way, she took a healthy interest in food. As in most other things. Although a non-driver, she was alive to foolishness on the road, always ready with an apt comment. And yet that morning, on the way into town, three glaring instances of dangerous stupidity on the part of rival motorists had gone not only unremarked upon by her, but seemingly unnoticed. Stephanie was beginning to feel real concern. Allowing an interval of a few moments, she altered tack.

'How's Simon?'

Again, Jo drifted back to within hailing distance. 'Fine.'

'No qualms about having his mother-in-law as a neighbour?'

'If he has, he's keeping them to himself.'

'And anyway, if he had,' Stephanie persevered, 'he'd hardly be likely to press ahead so enthusiastically with the annexe, would he?'

For an instant she thought she had lost her friend once more. But Jo, forking up a mouthful of prawns in a way more dutiful than ravenous, did offer a response, if something less than a relevant one.

'When we first got married, Simon and I used to have the most frightful arguments.'

'Me too, with Bob,' Stephanie said blankly, having waited vainly for a development of the topic. 'We still do. I could slay him sometimes.'

Jo glanced up at that. Presently she said, 'Common experience, I expect.'

'You bet.'

'The odd thing is, though . . .' Jo pondered for a second. 'More often than not, Mother tended to side with him over whatever it was we were rowing about. I quite resented it, sometimes.'

'Positive discrimination.'

'What?'

'Inverted impartiality,' explained Stephanie. 'Your mother was so keen not to seem to take sides in your favour, she went to the other extreme.'

'Oh. Maybe.'

'Or else she was just determined to avoid having a hostile son-in-law. Perhaps she's overdone it.'

'How do you mean?'

'Well, Simon seems quite set on the idea of this extension of yours, doesn't he? As if he can't wait to have your mother around. Could it be that he misses her even more than you do?'

The question was intended half-jocularly; Stephanie was

a little taken aback when Jo seemed to take it seriously. 'I don't know . . . I'm not sure. He's certainly been very good about the whole thing. Perhaps he does miss her, in a way.'

It was almost, thought Stephanie, as though her friend were trying to convince herself. 'I expect,' she suggested, to keep the conversation going, 'Simon comes up against plenty of hassle in the course of his work. He probably likes to unburden himself at home. And a sympathetic in-law can sometimes fit that sort of bill very nicely.'

'You could be right.' Jo was speaking from a distance again. Stephanie puffed inwardly. Dialogue with her friend was not normally an uphill task.

'Speaking of Granger's . . . what's the latest on the check-out supervisor who vanished? Any word of her yet?'

Jo picked up her glass of water and took a sip. 'Nothing.'

'Does Simon have any theories?'

'I wouldn't know.'

Stephanie studied her covertly. 'Friend of yours, wasn't she? I don't suppose you feel like talking about it.'

Jo turned her head to gaze again at the pierhead. 'There doesn't seem much point in talking about it. She's gone. The police think she might have hitched a lift out of the district, under stress or something. It's anybody's guess.'

'In a case like that,' Stephanie agreed, 'all anyone can do is guess.'

'It's coming along,' remarked Simon.

Inserting another stitch into the hem of the skirt she was shortening, Jo paused to wipe her fingers on a paper tissue. The July heatwave was showing no sign of abating. Clad in nothing but blouse and shorts, she still felt suffocated. 'So it should be.' To cover the listlessness in her voice, she raised the hem to study it for line. 'There's been nothing to hold them up.' She stirred herself to an effort. 'What stage are they at?'

'Haven't you been out there to see?'

'I've been a bit snowed under today.'

Simon, who continued to wear a necktie despite the temperature, made a faintly irritable tutting sound. 'Well, they'll be pouring the concrete into the base trenches tomorrow', Fenshaw tells me.'

'And when it's set, they can start building up?'

'That's the general idea.'

Recapturing the needle, Jo worked the point of it through the skirt material and pulled the thread taut, devoting as much concentration to the action as if she had been embroidering a portrait. Simon moved restlessly. 'You don't sound that interested.'

'I'll be interested when it's finished.'

'You mean, when your mother can move in?'

'That's the object of the exercise, isn't it?'

'I know of no other,' he said lightly.

The *Beacon* claimed his attention for a few moments. Refolding the newsprint presently, he draped it on the back of the sofa. 'Nothing in tonight about the case. They seem to have dropped it.'

Jo stitched on.

'I've not spoken to Dean since last Wednesday.' Simon put his feet up on the cushions. 'Have you?'

She squinted at the hemline. 'Why would I have spoken to him?'

'I just thought . . . Forget it. They're running the inquiry down, I imagine. Can't have the manpower to chase it up indefinitely.'

The thread snapped. Hunting inside her workbasket, Jo snipped off a fresh length from the reel, held the eye of the needle up to the light from the window while she rethreaded. Simon watched the operation. Although the necktie was still in place, on his arrival home he had changed into lighter slacks and exchanged his formal shoes for sneakers. With his fair hair sprawling a little at the front, he resembled a somewhat outdated teenager starting a holiday. As manager of a supermarket, he sometimes complained that his incurably boyish appearance was tantamount to a handicap, and at one time he had tried growing a moustache; the effect, however, had not satisfied him. Jo had always told him it didn't matter. It was personality that counted, not appearance.

'Why don't you use a sewing-machine?' he asked.

'I find this more relaxing.'

'You don't sound relaxed.'

'Should I be?'

Simon frowned. 'I can't think of any reason why not. We're in the clear, you know. Nothing whatever to worry about.'

'They'll be back. Asking questions.'

'It doesn't *matter*. I keep telling you. As long as there's no trace—and there won't be—they can interrogate from now till Christmas and it'll get them nowhere. Can't you get that into your thick skull?'

She looked up. 'What happens when someone at the apartment block lets slip that they've seen a man going into the flat with her? They will. Somebody always sees.'

A hiss of exasperation came from him. 'For the umpteenth time—nobody ever saw me go into the flat with her. Or even occupy the same lift. For the simple reason that I always hung back, followed her in later.'

'But you did go in. Someone's sure to have spotted you.'

'They might have noticed *a man*.'

'Disguise can be fairly futile.'

'If the police asked for a description,' Simon said, as if explaining arithmetic to a child, 'what would they get? A fellow in cap and glasses, glimpsed on a shadowy staircase or landing, probably from the side or rear. Have you any idea how murky that apartment block is? Even in daylight? The stairwells don't have windows. As for the lamps, they give a faint glow, that's all, and half the time they don't work. If anyone could recognize me as the person who went there a few times, they must have infra-red vision.'

'Your car could have been seen outside.'

'Assuming that someone was inquisitive enough to note the number . . . yes, I guess it could. If it was ever there. As it happens, it wasn't. I always parked a couple of streets away—never in the forecourt.' Simon took a righteous breath. 'I did have some regard for discretion.'

The thread entered the needle's eye. Securing it, Jo re-embarked on the hem, stabbing in stitches with nervy movements of her fingers.

'You thought of everything.'

'I'm not trying to justify what I did,' Simon said reasonably. 'But we both know it happened. Why not take comfort, now, from the fact that I was so cautious? It's working in our favour.'

'Until they find her.'

'They won't.'

'How can you be positive?'

Her eyes met his, challenging him. His frown deepened into a scowl.

'It's not important how. What counts is that I am. Good grief, Jo. You know how I feel about Carol. My one aim is to shield her from scandal and a broken home. So I'm not likely, am I, to slip up on this? Trust me.'

'The smartest people can trip.' Baiting him had become a compulsion, like picking at loose skin. 'Bodies have been buried, thrown down mine-shafts, sunk in lakes . . .'

'I read the newspapers, too.'

'Do you learn from them?'

'Yes. I learn how not to do things.'

Jo pricked her finger with the needle. Wincing, she sucked the flesh. Simon rose from the sofa. 'What time do I have to fetch Carol?'

'About now. Simon, before you go . . .'

'When I come back, I'll be doing a spot of gardening. It's too nice an evening to waste.' He strode from the room.

*

As the closing bars of Strauss's *Death and Transfiguration* Overture faded into silence, Jo uncurled herself from the armchair and flicked off the radio before the voice of the announcer could intrude. Leaning back again, she remained for a few moments staring out at the evening sky.

The setting sun had given a rosy topping to the Downs. Against the glow, a few hang-gliders continued to drift and gyrate, seizing the dying minutes of the day. As she watched, one of them came in at low altitude, hugging the end boundary of the garden before soaring again on an upcurrent and wheeling off back towards the hills. They were getting cheekier. Action of some kind, she thought cloudily, would have to be taken, before the incursions became an epidemic.

Hauling herself out of the chair, she hobbled stiffly from the room—keeping her gaze averted as usual from the armchair in the opposite corner—and mounted the stairs to the attic. Carol had arrived home from ballet class in a state of elation. The teacher had singled her out, asked her to perform a few solo steps in demonstration to the others, had afterwards taken her aside to offer a special tip or two. And finally had asked whether Carol intended making a career as a ballerina. Too excited to eat, Carol had spent the evening practising on her points in the spare bedroom, desisting only when fatigue took a hand and floored her suddenly, enabling Jo to wheel her off to bed before the start of the symphony concert on Radio Three. It was an hour since she had retired. Now, unaccountably, Jo felt a sense of uneasiness about her: she felt that she should have looked in on the child sooner, not left her with a hasty kiss before returning downstairs to lose herself in the world of music. Lately, she seemed to have been agonizing about Carol all the time. There was no reason for it. She just couldn't help herself.

The sight of the huddled shape on the bed brought her temporary reassurance. Carol had thrown off everything but the sheet and was hunched on her side, breathing deeply, oblivious of everything. Restoring one of the blankets gingerly to position, Jo left it loosely tucked in and tiptoed to the dormer window, which was half-open. Pushing it wide, she secured it with the metal stay against the soft probings of the breeze that was stealing in from the coast. She stayed there a moment, letting it fan her face.

From the window, which faced west, not south, only a part of the garden was visible. The area in view was heavily shaded by an adjoining belt of trees. Glancing down into it, Jo saw Simon. Wearing gardening gloves, he was trudging towards the side of the house in a stooped attitude. He seemed to be dragging something.

Drawing back a little, Jo craned her neck. Simon by now had moved further to her right and she could see more clearly. The thing he was dragging was black, sausage-shaped, apparently of substantial weight. With both hands about one end, he was hauling it across the grass in the direction of the extension site, which was hidden from her by the angle of the roof. As she watched, he and his burden passed jerkily out of sight.

Returning to the first floor, Jo ran a tepid bath and immersed herself for nearly an hour. When she emerged, the house was dark. Simon had come in from the garden; she could hear him moving downstairs. Preparing silently for bed, she switched off the light in their room and lay down, persisting stubbornly with the deep breathing that had helped to reduce her pulse-rate to something approaching normal as she reclined in the soothing water, soaping herself mechanically and repeatedly. Already she felt sticky again. Sleep was as distant as ever when at last the bedroom door slid open to admit Simon. While he undressed stealthily in the darkness, she feigned unconsciousness. The springing of the other bed grated a little as he committed his weight to the mattress. Outside in the garden, a hedgehog squealed.

CHAPTER 16

'Very grateful, Mrs Pettifer. Three with sugar, one without.'

'Shall I put the tray on the step, here?'

'That'll do nicely. I'll carry it round to the lads. Getting along a treat, they are. Pouring in the base aggregate, see, for the footings. Once they're *in situ*, we'll be well away.'

A lantern-jawed man of middle years, Alex Fenshaw had a punctilious manner which suggested an anxiety to keep his clients informed on every phase of the construction process, coupled with a conviction that everything he confided to them would pass directly through their heads to disperse harmlessly in the hollows of technological ignorance. 'While the fine spell lasts,' he added, giving grave attention to the cups Jo was sweetening and the one she wasn't, 'we're shoving on as fast as we can, like. Can't depend on the weather, not in this trade. Still, though, if we go on as we are, you should have your mother here by the early part of October, at the latest. How does that suit you?'

'Very well, thank you.' Jo replied with normal courtesy, although the meaning of what he had said had failed to register with her. Somewhere at the top of her brain, she knew that he was being kind and informative, and from habit she responded accordingly. 'I've put a tin of biscuits on the tray,' she said, picking it up to give it an experimental shake. 'Your men probably get hungry. How far down have you had to go?'

'Beg pardon?'

The question had slipped out, unplanned, a total surprise to herself. She stumbled for a moment. 'The footings . . . I suppose that means the foundations . . . how deep do they have to . . . ?'

'For a structure this size? Moderately substantial.'

Fenshaw paused to re-examine the phrase; finding it to his liking, he repeated it. 'Moderately substantial. Enough to prevent subsequent movement. You've a mixture of chalk and clay hereabouts, so . . .'

'Does that create problems?

The builder eyed her with some amusement. 'If you don't mind me saying so, Mrs Pettifer, you're a bit like your husband. While we was working on the Granger's job last year, he took a fair bit of interest in the technical side. Problems? Nothing the digger couldn't handle. It's not all elbow-grease nowadays, you know. Dear me, nothing like that. We've diesel-driven this and power-assisted that to fall back on, when it comes to earth-shifting. These lads of mine, they don't know they're born. Having said that, they're good workers, all three of 'em. So now I'll take 'em their reward.' Fenshaw picked up the tray. 'Leave it back here, shall I, when we're done?'

'That'll be fine.'

She watched him disappear round the corner of the house with the refreshment for his workforce. Presently the bellow of the concrete-mixer shut off. A laugh or two came from the site. That would be George, the resident humorist. Jo had been introduced to George, a plump Sussex thirty-year-old with a bottomless fund of stories and the facial gravity of the born comedian. Why were all such characters called George?

Turning, Jo walked slowly back into the house.

The concrete-mixer had been active again for half an hour when, above the din, the dual note of the doorbell reached the kitchen.

To give herself recovery time from the shock—any sudden noise now was nerve-jangling—Jo sluiced her floury fingers under the hot tap and dried off with a length of paper towel. Purposely she took her time. Crumpling the dampened tissue into a ball, she dropped it into the wastebin, smoothed down her overall. At a restrained pace she walked down the hall to the porch.

The man who stood there had his back to her. Beyond him at the head of the drive was parked an extremely racy soft-top car—Mercedes?—which seemed to be the object of his scrutiny, unless he was surveying the general layout of the front garden. Jo coughed.

'Yes? Can I help you?'

In leisurely manner he came round. 'If you're Mrs Pettifer, you might be able to.'

The accent was northerly. He looked to be in his late twenties and there was a burly, flush-necked, assertive look about him that was not restful. Without troubling to disguise the action, he looked her up and down. She swallowed hard.

'That's me. What can I do for you?'

'I'm making some inquiries about Polly Gathercole.'

'Chief Inspector Dean has already—'

'I'm not from the police. I'm her brother.'

'I *see*. Do come in, then, won't you? Can I offer you something?' I usually have a sherry about this time.'

'Scotch for me, thanks.' He stepped into the hall.

'To be perfectly truthful,' she said, leading the way, 'I wasn't aware that Polly had a brother. But then of course, we weren't *that* closely acquainted. You must be so worried about her, Mr Gathercole. I do hope she turns up soon. Anything with your whisky? Just a little water? There you go, then. Do sit down and ask me whatever you want.'

Ignoring the invitation, he remained standing in the centre of the room, examining the furniture in the same way as he had appraised the garden. He wore a smartly-tailored, lightweight suit of pale grey, with collar and tie, and his dark hair was groomed short. He looked like a young man who knew his way around. He looked back at her.

'This the scene of the meeting?'

'I'm sorry?'

'Where you sat talking with Dolly—my sister. She came

here that night to talk, didn't she? So I'm led to understand.'

'Naturally we talked. It was a social occasion. We've told the police all we can remember. Probably they've told you?'

'I've been speaking to them, yes. I've also talked to your husband. Simon.' The name was appended, not as an afterthought but for some more specific reason that for the moment Jo found elusive. Adding water to the Scotch, she took it across to him.

'Have you? He didn't mention that.'

'I suppose men don't always mention everything to their wives.' Clive paused deliberately. 'Where exactly was my sister parked down, while she was here?'

'That chair over there.' She nodded towards it. 'I don't know if you've any theories yourself, Mr Gathercole, about what might have become of Polly? It's so baffling. Simon and I—'

'I do have theories, yes. Mostly about what *didn't* become of her.'

'I'm afraid I don't quite—'

'For example, I don't believe she went off and disappeared, for no reason. Not Dolly. Not my sister.'

Jo returned steadily to the dresser to pour a drink for herself. 'But it does seem to be the only feasible explanation. A mental lapse of some kind. Surely we have to accept that?' The sherry bottle slipped a little, splashing the dresser surface.

'If I accepted it, I wouldn't be here.' He stood holding the whisky glass to his chest, staring out at the garden, before turning slowly to face her. 'How would it be, Mrs Pettifer, if I were to put my cards on the table, fair and square?'

'If you did, I could probably be more helpful.'

'You see, the day before Dolly was coming to see you, I had quite a chat with her. And everything was roses then. All going for her. She'd no reason to take off.'

'Maybe not, but—'

'She was going to call me next morning, describe how the meeting had gone. Only she never did.'

Jo mopped up the spilt sherry with a paper napkin. 'You talk rather as if it was some kind of head-on confrontation rather than a social visit.'

'Frankly, that was the impression I got.'

'Well, I'm afraid your impression is at fault. It was a perfectly routine, straightforward—'

'Look, Mrs Pettifer. Shall we stop fencing? In the first place, I don't believe that you and Dolly were ever buddies. If you had been, she'd have told me. I don't believe you ever met at the hairdresser's. I think you met for the first time when she came here that night.'

'You've absolutely no—'

'And in the second place, I'm prepared to bet that the relationship between her and your husband was more than a strictly social one.'

'Of course it was. They worked in the same supermarket, manager and employee.'

'I don't think you're as naïve, Mrs Pettifer, as you're trying to make out.'

'Naïve?'

'Your husband Simon was having an affair with my sister, wasn't he?'

'That's ludicrous.'

'So just what happened, that night she came here? You sat around, the three of you, exchanging pleasantries and swigging coffee? Don't give me that. There was more to it . . . or do I mean less?'

'I think you'd better leave.'

'Same as Dolly did? Walk out of the house, drive off? Is that the way the evening wound up?'

Jo wanted to sit down. As a diversion, in case he remarked upon the uncontrollable shaking of her knees, she planted her sherry glass heavily on the dresser and allowed it to knock against a cut-glass fruit bowl, producing a ringing sound.

'I'm truly sorry, Mr Gathercole, about your sister. Obviously it's upsetting for you, not knowing where she is. You've every right to feel agitated. But there are limits. To storm in here and accuse us of . . . Just what are you accusing us of?'

'All I'm after, right this minute, are replies to a few questions.' Clive ticked them off on long, thick fingers. 'What did you talk about that night? What was the outcome? When Dolly left here, was it under her own steam and was she in good nick?'

'We chatted over coffee, then she left in her Fiesta. That's all I know.'

'I don't believe you, Mrs Pettifer. Tell me where she is now.'

'I haven't a clue where she is.'

'Look. I told you. I talked to Dolly the day before her visit here. She said she was going to see this bloke she was going with, and his wife. She was planning to exert a bit of pressure. That's what she told me.'

'What does that have to do with us?'

'She also mentioned the name of her lover-boy. Simon. Your husband's called Simon.'

'It's a fairly common name.'

'Still . . . The odds mount up, wouldn't you say?'

'You would, apparently.'

'You're doing your damnedest to be loyal to your husband, Mrs Pettifer. That I respect. But look at it from my viewpoint. I'm desperate to know where Dolly is—to know that she's safe. Say it was a brother of yours: you'd feel the same, wouldn't you? So please, level with me. I'll keep any confidence you want observed. Can't say fairer.'

Jo walked to the door. 'There's nothing more I can tell you, Mr Gathercole. Please go now.'

Clive placed his glass carefully alongside hers on the

dresser. 'If that's the way you want to play it . . . Okay. I believe you're making a big mistake, but it's your decision.'

'It certainly is.' Opening the door, she stood clear to give him access to the hall. 'Forgive me for hurrying you off, but I do happen to be a little busy at present. We've got the builders in.'

'So I noticed.' Back inside the porch, he paused to listen to the hubbub at the side of the house. 'Mixing concrete, by the sound of it.' He rotated suddenly to look at her, causing her to retreat a pace. 'Messy business, having men in. You'll be glad to see the back of them. On the other hand . . .' He listened again. 'They do get things done, don't they? They're a means to an end. Don't wait, Mrs Pettifer, to see me off. I'm sure you've more important things to do.'

'Who was that man, Mummy, in the big car?'

'An acquaintance of Daddy's. What are you doing home, darling, this time of day?'

'There was a fire,' Carol explained laconically, 'in the school canteen. They couldn't cook anything, so they sent us home for lunch.'

'They might have warned parents. Who brought you back?'

'Vanessa's mother. She's got a Range-Rover. It's super. She's calling for me again at quarter to two.'

'You mean she dropped you outside, not knowing if I was here or not?'

'We saw you. Standing in the porch with that man. He stared at me as he went by. What can I have to eat?'

'I don't know. You've caught me on the hop. Poached egg?'

'All right. I'm just going to see what the builders are doing . . .

'No, dear. Not now.'

'Why not?'

'You'll make yourself untidy before you eat. Besides, they

won't want you getting in their way. They'll be stopping for lunch themselves soon, I expect.'

'I wanted to watch them emptying the cement in the holes. There's masses of it.'

'Yes, well . . . All the more reason for staying out of their way.'

'He can't know.' Simon steadied Jo by the arm as they negotiated the sunbaked ruts of the lane. 'He can only make guesses.'

She moved her arm away. 'That's more than enough to be going on with.'

'Stop sweating. There's nothing he can do.'

'He's her brother. He won't let up.'

'So? He's beating his head against a stone wall. The only people who matter are the police, and they've virtually written it off as a missing person riddle. They're not going to undertake all kinds of fresh investigation, just because Clive Gathercole tells them to.'

'How do you know?'

'He'd need new evidence.'

'Maybe he's got some.'

'I'd like to know what it is.'

'And there's something I'd like to know.' Halting at the blind top of the lane, Jo gazed up at the Downs before turning, setting off back towards the house. A cow in an adjoining field, watching them impassively over a thorn hedge, swatted flies robotically with its tail.

'What is it?'

'Do I have to spell it out again?'

'Drop it, Jo. Through not knowing, you were able to fob him off that much more convincingly today—right? That's the way we want it. That's the way it's going to be.'

'Even if I'm driven off my rocker?'

'Don't let yourself be.'

'That's easy to say. As things stand, I just spend my

whole time imagining things. It could reach the stage where I blurt something out, simply because I've lost touch with reality. Is that what you want?'

'I know you better than that.'

'You can think you know people. I thought I knew you.'

Simon was silent. The ruts levelled out into the stony surface that led up to their rear gate, a five-barred affair which he held half-open while she passed through. Securing it behind them, he pursued her to the edge of the lawn.

Here, he made a remark. 'Grass needs cutting.'

'I'd have thought,' Jo said caustically, 'you could have done it last night.'

'Why last night?'

'You were out here long enough.'

'Had other things to see to first.'

'Yes, I'm sure you did.' She could hear hysteria rising to the surface of her own voice. Simon blinked at her.

'There's an acre to be seen to, for God's sake. It's a question of priorities.'

'Since you're so pushed for time, wouldn't it be better to get on with things instead of wasting time when you get home, talking to Fenshaw and inspecting progress?'

'We're paying through the nose for Fenshaw. I like to keep an eye on what he's done.'

'I can tell you what he's done. He's concreted the foundation trenches.'

'I know that.'

'Good. Does it make you happy?'

'I can't think what's got into you,' Simon said, after a pause. 'You seem to be working yourself up to a fit over nothing. Get a hold on yourself, Jo. Just let yourself believe that I know what I'm doing.'

He walked off across the turf. Staring after him, clenching her fists until they ached, she felt the compulsion mount inside her: she craved a warm bath, soap, sponges, flannels. It was a call that could not be denied. Waiting until he had rounded the corner beyond which lay the extension site, she made hurried tracks for the patio door. Above her, almost vertically overhead, a hang-glider hovered, to all appearances motionless like a waiting hawk. Undeniably, this time, he was crowding their airspace, but she was in no mood to consider methods of making an official complaint: she had other calls upon her attention.

'So, what do you reckon?' Making a final check of the stowage of his gear on the car trailer, Mike Welling looked across hopefully at his friend and hang-gliding associate, Charles Lee, whose own car was parked alongside. 'Should I talk to someone about it?'

'The cops, you mean?'

'Who else, bonehead?'

'I thought you were asking. If you've already made up your mind . . .'

'I've not. I don't want to make myself look a Charlie.'

'Thanks a lot.'

'Nothing personal intended. It's just that I could be adding two and two together and making thirty. Besides which, I was drifting where I shouldn't at the time. I don't want to stir up trouble for myself.'

His friend looked contemplatively out over the twilit Sussex Weald spread below them. 'If you did happen to provide a useful tip-off, I'm sure they'd wink at your methods. I'd give them a call, if I were you.'

CHAPTER 17

The car grabbed Carol's attention as she approached the sweetshop.

The converted front room of a tile-hung cottage, the sweetshop stood at the farther end of the village from the school, but pupils had permission to visit it during the lunch-hour as long as they kept strictly to the footpath on that side and limited themselves to three in the shop at any one time: more than this, and old Mrs Weaver who ran the place was apt to lose her head and threaten violence. Today, Carol had found nobody to accompany her. Lynda's pocket money had expired the day before. Vanessa, who had just had a tooth filled, was banned from confectioners until further notice. When Carol arrived, two boys from the school were there ahead of her, and so she loitered outside while they made their choices. She liked a clear field, herself.

Under cover of inspecting the shop window contents, she aimed a second glance at the car. It was parked illegally in the bus lay-by outside the Ploughman's Arms, thirty yards from the sweetshop on the other side of the road, and what had particularly caught her notice was its colour: a rich crimson, with twin parallel silver lines encircling the body-work at door-handle level to culminate in a crest at the front. Carol approved of vivid hues in a motor vehicle. They were sensible, in her opinion, because you could see them coming; furthermore, they added a cheerful splash to the scene. On top of which, she was sure she recognized the car. She had seen it two days previously, parked at the head of the drive when she arrived home unexpectedly for lunch.

As the two boys emerged from the shop, Carol darted inside. She had fifty pence to spend, given to her that morning by her father, apparently on a whim. Lately he had done something of the kind on several occasions, dishing out cash and kisses as though anxious to compensate for something. Making her answer the policeman's questions, perhaps. But that had been nothing. More bothersome, to Carol, was her mother's faintly erratic behaviour, something new in her experience. She wanted to demonstrate solidarity, which was why she had visited the sweetshop. The purchase she was about to make was not for herself.

Mrs Weaver was shuffling jars at the back of the shop.

Eyeing the shelves, Carol cogitated. Soft centres. They were the main attraction. Most of the boxes on display, however, held assortments, and these always seemed to include a preponderance of teeth-splintering interiors that Carol would have hesitated to feed to a dog. Anyhow they were beyond her pocket. Even a modest bar, filled or solid, would have swallowed up her fifty pence and more.

Discouraged, she lowered her sights to the novelties. One or two of these were affordable, but none of them seemed much to present to a parent. Choosing for others, she concluded, was tricky.

'Something you were looking for, dear?'

Shyly, Carol showed old Mrs Weaver her coin. 'Have you got anything for that?'

'How about these? They've got toffee in them. Or this—it's a kind of brittle. This jar here—'

'I mean something chocolatey. With cream inside.'

'Chocolate, with cream . . .' Mrs Weaver began myopically to rummage. Carol watched hopefully. She still half-expected the occasional miracle from adults, despite regular disillusionment. Presently, true to form, the shop-owner began shaking her head. 'The nearest we've got, love, is the fondant candy at sixty-four. Can you run to that?'

Desolately, Carol shook her head.

'I'll take a couple of those.'

The voice boomed above her. Mrs Weaver looked up with the professional smirk she allocated to grown-ups. 'Two of the fondants, sir? That'll be one-twenty-eight.'

'And five Panatellas.'

'Three-ninety. Thank you, sir.' Bearing his five-pound note to the till, Mrs Weaver squinted over the keys, fingertips poised. The newcomer smiled down at Carol.

'They're good,' he informed her, jabbing a thumb at a gold-wrapped packet.

She said impulsively, 'Are you a policeman?'

'Sort of a policeman.'

'I thought you were. I saw you at my house the other day.'

'That's right. I was there.'

Mrs Weaver returned with change which she counted into his palm. 'Tenpence is four pounds, and a pound is five. Something else for you?' There was reserve now in her manner. Carol had noticed this occur before, with other acceptable-looking adults. The mood changes of Mrs Weaver were a constant source of perplexity. This time Carol felt annoyed, into the bargain. The man was a policeman and he had spoken to her mother: he must be all right.

'Nothing, thanks.' The sudden faint hostility seemed to have passed over him. Thrusting the cigars and one of the candy bars into a side pocket, he slapped the other down in front of Carol. 'For you, young lady. Compliments of the Force.' Turning, he strode out of the shop.

Carol stared dazedly at the candy bar, then looked up. 'Does he mean I can have it?'

'He left it there for you.' Mrs Weaver spoke brusquely. Her mouth was a thin line. Through the window, she watched the man's retreating figure as he headed for the crimson car in the lay-by. 'It's paid for. You'd better take it . . . but wait here, dear, till he drives off. Then go *straight* back to school—promise? Don't stop to talk to anyone. And if that gentleman—'

'I know,' Carol said scornfully. 'Mummy's told me. Anyhow,' she added, preparing for departure as they saw the car turning in the road, 'he *is* a policeman. He's been to our house.'

'Hallo, Mother. How are things?'

'Fine, this end.' Doris placed the tiniest emphasis on the middle word. 'I'm only calling to ask how you're feeling.'

'Me? I'm okay. Why shouldn't I be?'

'I thought you sounded not quite yourself, last time we spoke.'

'Can't think what gave you that idea.' Jo sought inspiration from the patterned wallpaper. 'We're all in the pink. Carol's been to ballet class twice this week. Her teacher says—'

'I'm not asking about Carol, dear. I'm asking about you.'

'For Heaven's sake, Mother. There's nothing wrong with me. I did have a touch of indigestion yesterday. Carol bought me a candy bar. But I'm fine now.'

'It's not your physical health I'm concerned about. Is anything niggling at you?'

'Of course not.'

'No second thoughts about me dumping myself on you?'

'You're not dumping yourself. We're inviting you.' Jo caught her breath. 'Incidentally, they've made a start on the brickwork. It's about a foot high, all round. You must come over and study progress.'

'All right, dear. Whenever's convenient. He sounds quite a good man, this builder of yours.'

Jo closed her eyes. 'He seems to believe in making a thorough job of everything. I suppose one can't complain about that.'

Chief Inspector Walter Dean accepted a sugarless coffee from the office machine and a custard cream biscuit from a Special Offer packet filched from the display shelves by Nigel Fielding. 'Never could resist one of these,' he remarked, biting off a corner. 'Especially when I'm on a case. I tend to get hungry. Just looked in, Mr Pettifer, to give you a rundown on events. Not, I fear, that there's much to report.' He chewed and swallowed. 'This disappearance of your Miss Gathercole is starting to take on the aspect of a classic puzzler. I'll be frank with you. I expected her to show up inside a couple of days: a week at the outside. I was wrong. She's melted into thin air.'

From behind his desk, Simon nodded. 'Have you managed to build up any sort of picture, Chief Inspector, of her possible movements after she returned to her flat?'

'Not *her* movements, I'm afraid.'

'Someone else's?' Nigel Fielding suggested alertly.

'Yes, but whether or not it's relevant . . .' Inspecting the residue of the biscuit, the chief inspector ran it between his teeth and commenced shredding. When it had been dealt with, he took two gulps of coffee and came up with a satiated gasp. 'We've been talking to the people in the apartment block. Talk about Fort Anonymous. They all seem to lead totally separate existences. But by dint of patient probing . . .'

Nigel said expectantly, 'You've found someone who saw her that night? Arriving or leaving?'

'No such luck. One or two of them, though, did come up with vague descriptions of a man who's been spotted occasionally in the lift or on the stairs. He doesn't seem to belong in the block. And—significantly perhaps—he's not been seen again since Miss Gathercole vanished. There may be nothing in it. But it's the only hint of a lead we've got.'

Simon leaned back in his swivel chair. 'What kind of man?'

'The faceless sort,' Dean said whimsically. 'Always seen in shadow, or half turned away, or from one dimly-lit landing to the next . . . never a clear sighting. The best detail came from a Miss Brent, who dwells on the third floor. She tells us she'd noticed this character on several occasions in the course of the previous few weeks. Each time, she said, he was wearing broad-rimmed spectacles and a close-fitting, peaked cap . . .'

'Sounds almost like a disguise,' exclaimed Nigel.

'It sounds,' Dean agreed avuncularly, 'remarkably like a disguise. Exactly the thought that occurred to us. Now, by itself, Miss Brent's information is no great shakes: but there's more. On the night that Miss Gathercole vanished, an HGV driver heading out of Southweald on the London road gave a lift to a hitchhiker.'

He paused. Nigel stirred in anticipation. 'Answering Polly's description?'

'Hardly. The hitchhiker was male. Medium height, slim, wearing an anorak . . . plus, a peaked cap and glasses. Sound familiar?'

'Well, yes,' said Nigel, disappointed. 'But there must be scores or hundreds of—'

'In the ordinary way I'd agree with you. Hundreds of similar men in similar outfits, you were about to say? You have to bear in mind, though, that it was a hot summer night—why a cap and anorak? The driver was in his shirt-sleeves with the cab window down, and sweating. As far as he can recall, the hitchhiker looked boiled as well, but he kept the cap on. Seems odd, to say the least.'

'Where did he take him?'

'Not far. The guy asked to be dropped off at the junction with the West Challerton road. Just said thanks and walked off into the night.'

Nigel sucked in his cheeks. 'What made the driver mention it to you?'

'He thought the incident seemed a bit offbeat, that's all. We'd put out an appeal for information from anyone who gave anyone else a lift that night, so he responded. He lives in Southweald himself, as it happens.'

Simon came forward in his chair. 'Where does the tie-up with Polly come in, Chief Inspector? I don't quite see . . .'

'There very likely isn't one,' Dean conceded breezily. 'We've made inquiries in West Challerton, but nobody there admits knowledge of a local with a peaked-cap-and-glasses fetish. Neither does anyone recall seeing a young woman of Miss Gathercole's description in the village at any time. Not that it necessarily signifies,' he added, coming to his feet. 'Even if she was involved with a man of that type, it's perfectly feasible that she never went near his home territory . . . if it is his territory. There's precious little certainty of that, either.'

'West Challerton,' Nigel said musingly. 'That's not far from you, Simon, is it?'

'About three miles.'

Dean cocked an eyebrow. 'Go there much, Mr Pettifer?'

'Not often. Occasionally on Sundays, for newspapers. Why?'

'I just wondered whether you'd ever happened to see this mystery individual yourself, wandering around the place.'

Simon smiled. 'Not at nine a.m. on a Sunday morning. Besides, if he was in disguise, as we're supposing, then nobody would remember seeing him, would they? In the ordinary way, he'd presumably look quite different.'

'*Touché*.' The chief inspector shot him a comical look as he went out of the door. 'Who'd be a detective?'

CHAPTER 18

It was while Carol was leaving the school canteen after lunch that she spotted her benefactor again. In conversation with Mrs Hammond, the head teacher, he was keeping pace with her towards the school gate. Carol nudged Lynda.

'That's him!'

'Who?'

'The man I was telling you about. The policeman. The one that gave me the candy.'

Lynda showed interest. 'What's he doing here?'

'I expect,' Carol said importantly, 'he's on a Case.'

Lynda giggled. 'P'raps Mrs Hammond's going to be arrested.'

As they watched, the head teacher turned and came back to her room at the end of the corridor, shutting the door behind her. The man lingered at the gate, peering along the mainstreet as if looking out for the hourly bus. On impulse, Carol said, 'I'm going to thank him.'

'Carol, you mustn't! We're not meant to—'

'I'm only going to say thank-you.' Carol scampered down to the gate. The man looked down at her vaguely. Suddenly she was tongue-tied. Imposing more of his poundage on top of the gate, he gave her a more attentive inspection.

'I know you, don't I? The young lady in the sweetshop. Enjoy the candy?'

'I gave it to my mum.'

'Big-hearted of you. Did *she* enjoy it?'

'Yes, thank you. Thank you very much for giving it to me.'

'My pleasure. You like it here? Nice school, is it?'

'Yes, thank you.'

'I'm thinking of sending my daughter here. That's why I came along. To suss it out.'

Although uncertain what he meant, Carol was reassured to learn that he had a daughter. 'What's her name?'

'Um . . . Maureen. She's just six. If she does attend here, maybe you can be a big sister to her. Unless you've a sister of your own, already?'

Carol shook her head. 'I've not got a brother, either.'

'Just you, and your mum and dad? I've met your mother, you know. A week or so back, up at your house. *And* I spotted you as I was leaving.'

'I saw you, too.'

'Did she tell you what I called about? No? It was just a few inquiries I had to make, concerning a friend . . .'

'Miss Gathercole?'

'That's it, Miss Polly Gathercole. I don't suppose you know anything about her yourself. Never even met her, probably.'

'I did see her.'

'You did?' He looked pleased. 'Well, I never. What did you think of her?'

Carol glanced doubtfully back at the schoolhouse. At the window of Mrs Hammond's room she could make out the fuzzy silhouette of the head teacher, lurking behind the glass. She spoke hurriedly. 'I only saw her for a minute. Mummy made me go back to bed.'

'Oh, tough luck. You didn't actually get to speak with Miss Gathercole, then?'

'She spoke to me. A little bit.'

'What about? Anything exciting?'

Carol hesitated. 'She did say they'd been having an argument.'

'An argument . . .' He echoed the words slowly, leaving Carol with the distinct impression that what he had really wanted to do was rap them out sharply. He gave her one of his easy smiles. 'Always doing that, aren't they—grown-ups? Quarrelsome bunch. Still, a good lively discussion never did any harm. As long as they didn't come to blows.'

She said breathlessly, 'While Mummy was taking me out of the room—'

'Carol! You're to come back here, at once.'

Mrs Hammond had reappeared at the schoolhouse entrance to brandish an arm at her. A faint grimace interfered with the man's features. 'I think,' he observed, stepping without haste away from the gate, 'you're wanted back in class. Tell Mrs Hammond I'm sorry to have kept you and explain to her, will you, that I was just telling you about my daughter Marjorie. I hope we'll be seeing each other again. 'Bye for now, Carol.'

Mrs Hammond was waiting with a rare scowl narrowing her eyes. 'Carol, what have you always been told?'

'Sorry, Mrs Hammond. I was just—'

'You are *not* to talk to strangers. Whoever it is, makes no difference. What was Mr Thomas saying to you?'

'He was telling me about Marjorie, Mrs Hammond.'

'You mean Maureen? His daughter?'

'He said Marjorie. Well, he did say Maureen at first.'

Mrs Hammond regarded her for a moment. 'Did he now?' she said drily. 'I suggest, dear, you forget about that daughter of his. I've a feeling she won't be joining us, somehow. Get back to the classroom now, and remember what I said. Oh, and Carol . . .'

'Yes, Mrs Hammond?'

'Are you feeling a little better?'

'I've not been ill, Mrs Hammond.'

'No, but I thought you've been looking a bit under the weather lately. Slightly down in the dumps.'

Carol gazed back at her. The head teacher gave her a quick smile. 'Perhaps I was mistaken. Don't hesitate to come to me, will you, if there's anything the least bit wrong?'

Strangely, Carol did start to feel increasingly out of sorts as the afternoon progressed.

It wasn't illness. At any rate, she thought not. She didn't feel sick, or have a stomach pain. What she felt was a headachey sensation coupled to an undertow of desolation: a conviction that something had been left unsaid or undone, something vital and yet shadowy, beyond her power to specify. The one thing she was sure about was that, until it was pinpointed, the stuffed-head feeling would refuse to go away.

Pressure seemed to be gathering behind her eyes, making them start out like those of a Pekingese. Strive as she might to relax them, blink them back into their sockets, the impression of protuberance remained.

During the mid-afternoon break she fully expected Lynda to comment upon her appearance. Either her friend was unobservant, however, or she herself was imagining things. Only she wasn't imagining it. She felt wretched. Eventually, Lynda did seem to rumble this. They were alone together in a corner of the playground and Lynda had been describing a televised dance sequence shown the evening before, when she broke off suddenly. 'Carol, you're not listening! You look all droopy.'

'I feel droopy.'

'Did Mrs Hammond tell you off?'

'She was a bit cross. She said I shouldn't have been talking to that man.'

'I told you.' Curiosity overcame Lynda. 'What did he say to you?'

'Nothing much.' Carol scuffed her shoes on the asphalt, softened by the July heat of the sun. 'His daughter might come to the school. She's six.'

'Is that all?'

'Why shouldn't she be?'

'No, stupid. I meant, is that all he said?'

'No, it wasn't.'

The denial burst from Carol, thrown up irresistibly by the forces building within her. Looking intrigued, Lynda waited silently. With a glance at the nearest group of their fellow-pupils, who were engrossed in their own activities, Carol turned to face the road. 'He asked me about Miss Gathercole.'

'The one who went missing?'

'Yes. Who did you think?'

'What did he want to know?'

'What she said to me.'

'I thought she never spoke to you?'

'Well, she did. When I came downstairs. She said, Why couldn't I stay? And then she said she'd been arguing. Daddy looked awfully cross. He had a red face. He shouted at Mummy.'

'Why? What had she done?'

'I don't think she'd *done* anything. He just wanted her to take me out of the room. She looked quite scared. She grabbed hold of me and pushed me out of the door.'

Lynda looked awestruck. 'Did she hurt you?'

'Only a bit. She pinched my arms.' Carol broke off, scanning the road through the village.

'Then what happened?'

'I don't know. I never came back downstairs.'

Lynda registered disappointment. 'So you didn't see her again? Miss Gathercole?'

'I didn't *see* her. But . . .'

'But what?' Lynda prompted, having waited in vain.

The cranial pressure was unbearable. In an attempt to relieve it, Carol shook her head several times, then clutched her friend's wrist. 'Promise you won't tell, Lynda?'

'Cross my heart.'

'I think Daddy might have hit her. She was calling out, and then as I was going out of the door I heard this noise, a sort of click, and after that she stopped. I'm sure he must have hit her.'

'Did your mum hear it, too?' asked Lynda, after a moment's digestive pause.

'I don't know. She never said anything. She brought me up some hot chocolate, and after that I fell asleep. I don't remember any more.'

'P'raps,' Lynda said judiciously, 'that's why Miss Gathercole went away. P'raps your dad told her to.'

'Yes, he might have done. Don't tell anyone, will you, Lynda? I don't want anyone else to know.'

'I did promise.'

The clink of metal upon breezeblock reached Carol's ears as she came up the drive. Taking a detour, she halted at the fringe of the site to watch the builders.

The inner skin of the cavity wall was now three or four feet high, and currently being added to at a brisk pace. Mr Fenshaw, laying blocks as assiduously as his men, spotted her and waved. 'Are we going fast enough for you?'

She replied politely, 'You've got on very well, haven't you?'

'Thank you, madam. We do try to oblige.'

George, the funny one, threw her a grin as she went on, rounding the house to enter by the patio door. The pressure inside her head had eased at last. If her mother could only be back to something like normal, the day would end on the highest note for weeks. With fingers crossed, Carol gained the cool sanctuary of the living-room. Her mother wasn't there, but she could hear her voice.

Perhaps she was speaking to Nan. A visit, Carol knew, had been mooted, although for some reason it kept being deferred. Walking over to the door, which stood ajar, she peeped through into the hall.

'What exactly did she say?'

With the receiver pressed to her ear, her mother was standing with her back to Carol, her free hand planted against the wall as if for support. Her shoulders were hunched. Carol's heart sank. She wanted to turn away, and yet somehow she felt impelled to remain, listening.

'I can't see anything in that.' Her mother's voice was firm and yet, in the oddest way, faltering. 'To a nine-year-old child, it could well have sounded like an argument. We were talking politics. What? Well, Mr Gathercole, you should know your own sister. The discussion might have got a bit heated, yes. But we soon—'

Carol shut the door.

She was removing school books from her leather carrier and distributing them over the dresser when her mother finally came in from the hall. She looked up casually. 'Was that Nan on the telephone?'

'Just an acquaintance. Hallo, darling. Reasonable sort of day?'

'Yes, thank you.' Carol submitted to a kiss. Her mother's cheeks were mud-coloured, ice-cold. Shocked by the phenomenon in the midst of a heatwave, the child recoiled, diverted her attention to sorting out the books. Her mother hovered.

'No upsets?'

Carol glanced up again. 'How do you mean?'

'I thought you were looking a little tense. You didn't have a disturbing encounter with anyone?'

A vague sense of injustice surged in Carol's chest. 'I'd tell you if I had.'

'I hope so.' After a moment's further hesitation her mother turned away, made for the door, still with that hunched look to her bearing. 'I'll be getting your tea,' she said quietly, and went out.

Guilt replaced Carol's momentary irritation. Her mother looked so unhappy—ill, almost—that she ached to run after her, throw both arms about her waist, demand to know what was the matter. But a powerful inhibition held her back. Something told her that such an action would gain no result. Sorting the books into three piles, she sniffed a little. Her headache was starting to creep back.

Later, on the lawn, her father came across to greet her. 'Hi, poppet. More practice? We'll see you at Covent Garden yet.'

She stopped twirling. 'What's the matter with Mummy?'

'Nothing's the matter with her.'

'Then why has she gone to bed?'

'She's only resting,' her father said mildly. 'Felt a bit knocked out, that's all. I expect the heat got to her.'

'She keeps asking me funny questions.'

Her father gave her a smile that was not quite a smile. 'What kind of funny questions?'

'About meeting people. All that.'

The smile hung on. 'So, what have you told her?'

'There isn't anything to tell.' Trying out a few more steps across the grass, she rounded a shrub before returning. The delay gave her time to decide that she didn't want to tell her father about Mr Thomas: not now. 'I've got to rehearse this some more, because we're doing it on Friday. Does it look all right?'

'To my untutored eye, it looks terrific. You'll have to give a command performance for your Nan, when she finally gets here. Seen the annexe? Getting on, aren't they?'

Fabricating an interest, she came to a standstill. 'How long will it take them now, Daddy?'

'Not too long. They're up to waist height already. By the time you break up, they should have the roof on.'

CHAPTER 19

Peering up at his assistant, Chief Inspector Walter Dean tossed him a notepad which the other deftly caught. 'Take a look at that.'

'What is it?'

'A rough-and-ready account of what was said to me last night, by our friend.'

Detective-Sergeant Eric Conway uttered a groan. 'Not Gathercole again?'

'I agree: the man's obsessed. It doesn't alter the fact, though, that he could be on to something. Much as I might disapprove—officially—of his methods.'

'How would you describe his methods?'

'Harassment,' Dean said promptly. 'You can't call it anything less. He's taking the law into his own hands and twisting it till it shrieks, and it's all highly reprehensible, and I'm trying like crazy not to notice.'

'Can I ask why, sir?'

'Because, Sergeant, it could bring results.' The chief inspector eyed his deputy benignly. 'Lesson in Detection, number three on the schedule. When relatives interfere, let 'em. Personal involvement can work wonders.'

'What are Lessons one and two?'

'Don't let your overlords catch you at it. They tend to have this odd passion for going by the book. Which explains, young Eric, why I've kept the Super sixty per cent informed, while keeping the other forty per cent to myself . . . for the moment. Just run your eye down that.'

The sergeant did so. Presently he redirected the eye at his superior. 'Waylaying a small girl . . . pushing it a bit, sir, isn't it?'

'More than somewhat,' Dean concurred cheerily. 'But he does seem to have managed it quite adroitly. And he did get something out of the child.'

'"An argument",' the sergeant quoted dubiously from the notepad. 'On the sketchy side, if that's all she told him.'

'It's more than she told me. I had the disadvantage of having her parents present: I could see she was tongue-tied. The point, Eric, is this. According to both of them, all they had with Polly Gathercole was a matey chat over the coffee-cups. No mention of a dispute. Now, their daughter—'

'To a girl of that age, a lively debate might seem like a quarrel.'

'One bears that in mind. Just the same, it's a straw in this particular wind that I can't afford to ignore. Too many unanswered questions are still drifting around. And on the subject of drifting, don't forget what Mike Welling told us.'

'The hang-gliding ace? We certainly can't overlook that. Again, though, his story is inclined to be on the speculative side. I mean, what he saw, or thinks he saw, at nine o'clock in the evening from a height of—'

'I'm not treating it as holy writ,' Dean said patiently. 'Taken in conjunction with other things, though, it's not insignificant, you've got to admit. If Pettifer really was hauling a bundle across his garden towards the extension site . . .'

'Could have been a mound of rubble he wanted to dispose of.'

'Absolutely. I give due weight to all this. At the same time, I keep an open mind.' Springing to his feet, the chief inspector paced restlessly to the opposite wall and back. 'I'd give my eye-teeth, Eric, to be able to tackle that daughter of theirs on my own. She knows something, I'm convinced.

Clive Gathercole reckons he was just on the point of getting something really crucial out of her when that dratted head teacher threw herself between them. Quite rightly, of course. But she was an infernal nuisance, for all that. Now, we've probably lost it for good. It might have made all the difference.'

Conway's dubiety intensified. 'Whichever way you look at it, sir, it's the word of a juvenile. Chancey.'

Dean returned to his chair to ponder the ceiling. 'If it took us anywhere,' he pronounced presently, 'I'd be happy to accept the risk. It's not as if we can be accused of harrying the girl. I've only questioned her the once, for Pete's sake. The rest of the time I've been nosing mainly in Pettifer's direction . . . but he's a bit like a cat. Just as you think you're getting close, he does a kind of body-contraction and squirms out of reach. Frustrating.'

'Still no confirmation of anything between him and Polly Gathercole?'

The chief inspector wagged a regretful head. 'Half-hints, semi-pointers . . . they're all we seem to have collected. If they were having an affair, they were keeping it well under wraps. He strikes me as the type. Have it away with an underling, but insist on total secrecy. Otherwise he might lose his precious job.'

'If anything did threaten him,' Conway surmised, 'he mightn't think twice about drastic action.'

'My view entirely.'

'How about his wife? Think she's in on a cover-up?'

'That's harder to answer. She impresses me as a nice woman. Would she be party to something criminal?'

'She might. If her home life was on the line.'

'How d'you mean, exactly?'

Conway lowered himself thoughtfully on to the desk. 'Suppose Pettifer and Polly Gathercole were having a fling, and she started to get demanding. Wanted him to divorce his wife and marry her. That doesn't suit his book—and it doesn't suit his wife's. She's all for the status quo. So, they invite the Gathercole woman along . . .'

'Why?'

'To talk it over.'

'Yes, but why? If the wife knows about it anyhow, and she's willing to have him back, what's the point of discussing anything with the mistress? All Pettifer need do is drop her and return to the fold.'

Conway cogitated, staring straight ahead. 'Polly,' he suggested, 'has something on Pettifer. Some racket at the supermarket . . . ? She can blow the lid on him. So, she has to be squared before things can revert to normal.'

'Only she refuses to be fobbed off.'

'So they get rid of her instead.' Conway relaxed his eye-muscles to glance interrogatively at his superior, who sat gently massaging the side of his nose before giving vent to a prolonged sniff.

'It's a theory.'

'It has to be something along those lines,' the sergeant argued. 'Assuming, that is, she *has* been got rid of, and they *are* responsible. Otherwise it makes no sense.'

'Few cases make sense,' Dean reminded him, 'until they explode in your face. You may be on the right track, Eric. I've been exploring it myself. But unless and until we—'

His telephone blurted. Grunting into the mouthpiece, he listened, lobbed a glance at Conway, listened again. Finally he said, 'Send her up, will you?' Cradling the receiver, he looked straight ahead for a moment. 'Stand by,' he said quietly. 'We've got a visitor.'

To Stephanie, the sergeant for all his bulk and drooping moustache and knotted eyebrows was by far the less formidable of the pair who confronted her in the first-floor room of the CID section to which she had been piloted. The smaller, chubbier man with the friendly, watchful eyes who had invited her to sit down, tell him what was on her mind, was the one to watch. She wished, more desperately than ever, that she hadn't come. But here she was, committed. Her mouth had to remain open, articulating sentences. She had no choice.

'I didn't want to say anything,' she told them, conscious of the echoes of her own voice in her ears. 'I detest the thought of it, quite honestly. Only I felt I had to—'

'Your position, Mrs Ross,' the chief inspector said solicitously, 'is one that we fully appreciate. You're a friend of Mrs Pettifer's. You feel disloyal.'

'I feel a traitor.'

'Try not to think about it that way. You're acting in the public interest—this is what counts. You say that Mrs Pettifer has been behaving a little oddly for some while?'

'Out of character.' Stephanie hesitated. 'We came on a shopping trip to Southweald last week, and I couldn't seem to get through to her. Normally she's so bright. This time she seemed miles away: it was a complete waste of a day. I've been waiting for her to get in touch with me since, but she hasn't. It's not like her.'

Dean nodded encouragingly. 'Anything else?'

'Oh yes. That's just incidental. What I really came in to tell you about was a talk I had with my daughter Lynda last night. We generally have a little chat before she nods off. She tells me things that she's hoarded during the day. She's not a tale-teller, I don't meant that. She simply—'

'I quite follow. What was it, last night?'

Stephanie tugged at the clasp of her shoulder-bag. 'Mind if I have a cigarette?'

'Please.' Offered the packet, Dean declined with a gesture, leaned across with a lighted match. Dragging in smoke, Stephanie felt spineless. What had become of her vow to abstain? This was her fifth of the morning, and it wasn't yet nine-thirty. She had driven into Southweald straight from delivering the girls to school, before she could change her mind.

'Lynda,' she resumed, tapping ash into the glass receptacle that Sergeant Conway slid to her across the desk, 'told me about a conversation she'd had with Jo's daughter, Carol. Yesterday afternoon, in the playground. Apparently, Carol seemed upset. She'd been talking to a man at lunchtime.'

'A man,' Dean said neutrally.

Stephanie glanced up. 'I don't think it was anything . . . like that. According to Carol, he asked her about Polly Gathercole, and Carol told him that on the night of Miss Gathercole's visit she came downstairs—Carol did—and found them arguing. She said her father was red in the face and shouting at her mother, who looked scared.'

Stephanie took another pull at the cigarette. Dean and Conway exchanged glances.

'Was that all she said, Mrs Ross?'

'No, it wasn't. She told Lynda: '*I think Daddy hit her.*'

'Hit who?'

'Miss Gathercole. Jo and Carol were leaving the room at the time. Carol said she heard a noise and Miss Gathercole's voice stopped—just cut off. She was quite definite about it.'

The chief inspector sat motionless. 'Did she say anything else?'

'Carol? No, but she made Lynda promise not to tell anyone. Which by her own lights,' Stephanie added defensively, 'she didn't. I'm not included in the "anyone". I'm her mother. That's different.'

'My own daughter,' said Dean briskly, 'would have reasoned exactly the same at Lynda's age. One further point, Mrs Ross. Apart from Mrs Pettifer, you've had no opportunity, I suppose, to observe the recent behaviour of her husband?'

Stephanie gulped. 'I've not actually set eyes on him lately. But one thing has struck me. He's having this annexe built for Jo's mother . . .'

'We know about it.'

'Well, it's all being done in a frantic hurry. He brought in a Hove builder who's got a reputation for fast work, and they seem to be going at it hammer and tongs.' She met the chief inspector's eyes. 'I just thought it worth mentioning.' Abruptly, Stephanie crushed the remainder of her cigarette into the ashtray and stood up. 'Would you mind if I go now? It's been something of an ordeal.'

After a snatched lunch, Sergeant Conway reported back to find the chief inspector closeted with the superintendent and a couple of inspectors, one of them the officer responsible for special technical projects. After the conference had broken up, Dean called him in.

'Right, Eric. We're in business.'

'Super happy about it, sir?'

'Hilarious. At least, he's putting a good face on it. I don't think he fancied shoving a spanner in the works and then possibly being made to look stupid later.'

'Neither do we, sir. Do we?'

Dean grimaced. 'I said I was willing to take a chance.'

'So . . . When do we move?'

'First light tomorrow. Keep your fingers crossed.'

CHAPTER 20

In common with its national counterparts, the *Beacon* carried an extensive account of the proceedings in its issue of July 16:

> Police searching for Polly Gathercole (30), the store check-out supervisor missing since June 23, yesterday visited a house near the small village of Melking and, with the aid of contractors' equipment, demolished an extension that was being built alongside it.

The house is occupied by the store manager, Mr Simon Pettifer, his wife, and their nine-year-old daughter. They were given no warning of the police action.

The surprise operation began at 5 a.m. when a team of police led by Detective Chief Inspector Walter (Wally) Dean, who is leading the hunt, arrived at the isolated converted farmhouse nestling at the foot of the Downs and set to work with sledgehammers, pickaxes and shovels.

Backing them up was a team of professionals who used pneumatic drills and mechanical diggers to shatter the walls and footings of the annexe—still in course of erection by a Hove firm of builders, Fenshaw's.

Chief Inspector Dean told the *Beacon*: 'As a result of certain information, a decision was taken to investigate the immediate area of the Pettifers' home extension, and in order to do this we are having to dismantle the construction work already done, which we regret. Depending on what we find, compensation will of course be available for the damage caused.'

Asked what he expected to unearth, the Chief Inspector replied: 'At this stage, we are keeping an open mind.' Excavation work, he added, would continue 'until we are satisfied that every part of the site has been thoroughly examined.' This, it was thought, might take at least a couple of days.

Police-constables, working in their shirtsleeves in the wake of the diggers, carefully sifted the subsoil and rubble beneath the annexe—intended for the use of Mrs Pettifer's mother. When the operation was suspended, late yesterday evening, nothing had been found except the carcase of a hedgehog deep below the concrete foundation of an outer wall.

Work was scheduled to resume this morning. It is believed there are also plans to investigate a septic tank near the perimeter of the garden.

While digging was in progress, Mr Pettifer remained

inside the house. His wife, Joanna, and daughter Carol, who attends St Peter's Church Primary School in the village, were driven away by minicab during the morning to an unspecified destination. Mrs Pettifer appeared to be in some distress.

At Granger's supermarket in Southweald, the assistant manager, Mr Nigel Fielding, told the *Beacon*: 'We are all a bit in the dark as to what is going on. All I know is, I received a telephone call early this morning from Mr Pettifer to say that he was unavoidably delayed at his home, and asking me to take over in his absence. He did not mention the reason for his being held up, although I gathered it had nothing to do with illness.'

Mr Fielding added that Mr Pettifer had recently been questioned on a number of occasions by the police in connection with the disappearance of Miss Gathercole, who had worked at the store for about a year as checkout supervisor.

'This, I understand, was because she had visited his house on the night she vanished, and it was hoped he might be able to shed light on the mystery. He was unable to, however.

'He told me he was completely baffled by Polly's disappearance.'

In its issue of July 17, the *Beacon* again led on the story and published a front-page picture of the site devastation.

Late yesterday afternoon, the police operation to demolish a 'granny flat' being built at the home of Mr Simon Pettifer near Melking was called off.

A team of twelve detectives, working in shifts for nearly two days in blazing sunshine, had reduced the site of the annexe to a heap of earth and rubble, but had found nothing of significance. At 5 p.m. the order was given for all equipment to be removed and the site vacated.

By 7 p.m., peace had returned to the house which for 48 hours had been at the centre of inquiries into the mysterious disappearance of supermarket employee Miss Polly Gathercole.

Mr Pettifer, her boss at Granger's Southweald store, told the *Beacon* he felt no resentment towards the police, even though by their action they had destroyed hundreds of pounds' worth of building work and had put back the completion date of the 'granny flat' by several months.

'They have their job to do,' he said, 'and I appreciate the reasons for the official interest that was taken in the construction work I was having carried out.

'Understandably, in all the circumstances, Chief Inspector Dean took the view that there were questions to be answered. I can only add that I am thankful this part of the investigation has now been concluded.'

Mr Pettifer's wife and daughter, who have been staying in a Southweald hotel, are returning to the house later today.

On the question of compensation, Mr Pettifer said this was something that would have to be thrashed out between his solicitor and the police. He expected an amicable settlement to be reached.

'My greatest regret,' he said, 'is that my mother-in-law, who we were hoping would take up residence before Christmas, will now have to wait until well into the New Year before she can move in. Luckily, however, she is not homeless in the meantime, and we shall just have to put up with the delay.'

The annexe would be rebuilt to the original design. 'I have promised this to my wife, and I hope that when the scheme comes to fruition it will make up to her and my daughter for this rather traumatic incident.'

CHAPTER 21

In Doris's estimation, her daughter was looking peakier than ever.

'You don't seem at all well, love,' she confided, while Simon, with Carol's assistance, was slotting the luggage into the Renault's stern. 'You're all puffy around the eyes. Aren't you sleeping?'

'I dream enough. So I must be asleep, mustn't I? I'm okay, really.'

'What do you dream about? Not that nasty business back in the—'

'No, no. Just the usual nonsense. If I look tired, it's probably because of Christmas. I'm never at my best in the run-up to all the jollity. How about you, Mother? Fingers still playing up?'

'They don't seem to improve much. Hurts to hold things.'

'How did you manage with the suitcases, the other end?'

'Young Graham from the flat upstairs, he ran me to the station and saw me on the train. Ever so sweet, he was. So obliging. Not like some of them nowadays.' Doris twisted in her seat. 'Getting on all right, back there?'

'Yes, Nan. It's nearly all in.'

'You'd think I'd come to stay for a month, not five days. You feel you have to bring the lot, just in case.'

'Don't worry. We've done the same.'

'How far is this hotel?' demanded Doris, who was still only partially reconciled to the notion of spending Christmas in commercial surroundings rather than cosily at home with the washing-up.

'Just at the back of the town, facing the Downs on the seaward side. I hope you like it.'

'You did, didn't you? You and Carol.'

'We were only there a couple of nights,' Jo said briefly.

'It suited you, though?'

'I wasn't taking much notice, at the time. Carol says she liked it. And this Christmas package of theirs seems exceptional value. We thought we'd give it a shot.'

'Save on the domestic chores,' explained Simon, occupying the driving seat and strapping on harness while Carol, alongside, virtuously did likewise. 'Also it'll get Jo away from the house. Give her a break.'

'It's a very nice thought, my dear.'

'Could turn out to be fun. They organize various things.'

'A party,' volunteered Carol, turning saucer-eyed to her grandmother, 'on Christmas Day. Presents from the tree and *everything*. And you don't have to pay for *anything*.'

'That's right,' Simon said wryly, launching the car from station forecourt to street. 'All on the house.'

'Talking of houses,' remarked Doris, craning her neck to catch a glimpse of the seafront, 'I'll miss not seeing your place, this trip. Seems funny, coming all this way and never going near.'

'You're not actually missing a lot. The builders are in full spate again—it's chaos. We're glad to be out of it.'

'Took their time, didn't they, getting stuck in again? If they'd started rebuilding directly after the police—'

'Two reasons for the delay,' Simon explained, braking to avoid a cyclist. 'First, Jo and I had a few second thoughts about the design. Since we'd been handed the opportunity, we changed the layout a bit and upped the dimensions, which meant submitting new plans to the council. Then when we got the go-ahead, Fenshaw's couldn't make a start at once because by that time they were involved with two other jobs . . .'

'Couldn't you have gone to another builder?'

'We could, but we liked Fenshaw's. They're a good, reliable outfit. So we decided to wait, but it was the end of last month before they were finally able to get back to us.'

'How are they getting on?' Doris inquired, after an interval.

Simon was preoccupied with traffic lights and a knot of vehicles at an intersection. It was Jo who answered, with a certain lack of spontaneity. 'Making headway. They've put in new foundations and they should be bricklaying soon. That's if the mild weather holds.'

'What if we get a freeze-up?'

'In that case,' said Simon, having cleared the entanglement, 'they'll just have to wait for the thaw. It's a crazy time of year to start a building job—restart it, that is—but we might be lucky. January can be quite balmy, sometimes.'

'Most of the Januaries I've known,' Doris announced uncompromisingly, 'were enough to freeze the blood in your veins. I'm sure that's what's given me arthritic hands. Those builders of yours had better watch out. They could be laying up trouble for themselves.'

The paper chains, balloons, silver thread and artificial snow with which the Crestview Manor Hotel had been heavily embellished had even found their way on to the reception desk and inside the lift. Carol was enchanted. She and the fatherly porter, who remembered her from July, exchanged badinage as he conducted them to their rooms on the third floor: a family four-bedder, plus an adjoining single for Doris. From the windows, a sliver of Downland could be discerned beyond a belt of rather dusty woodland and an office block. When they were installed and unpacked, Simon proposed tea in the hotel lounge.

They had the room to themselves. Today was Sunday, the day before Christmas Eve: no other guests had yet arrived for the package period. A waiter brought tea and pastries. Taking command of the trolley, Doris poured cupfuls for everybody, using both hands for the teapot, and began to feel a little festive.

'Bit of all right, this,' she observed to Carol, sinking back luxuriously into her fat, chintzy, profoundly upholstered armchair after selecting a cream slice from the dish. 'Makes a nice change, having it done for you.'

'You see?' Simon said to Jo. 'Your mother thinks along my lines. Didn't I say?'

She nodded while sipping, but said nothing. Doris wished she would liven up a bit. Obviously she was trying hard, but the mechanism creaked. Deciding for the moment against any sort of rallying cry, Doris turned to her granddaughter. 'Well, love? Picked up any new steps?'

Carol had, and she demonstrated a few. They all applauded, Simon most vigorously. 'She's so fast to cotton on,' he remarked to Doris, with the grave restraint of a parent finding it difficult not to talk in superlatives. 'In fact I've been wondering . . . Should she go on to one of the specialist schools, here in town, when she leaves the primary? Somewhere academic, only with a dance bias. I believe there are several. What do you think?'

Surprised and flattered to be consulted, Doris equivocated. 'Come a bit on the pricey side, don't they? Can you afford it?'

'We'd manage,' he said confidently.

If he didn't mind discussing it, Doris decided, she didn't either. 'I suppose you must be earning quite well now, Simon, down at Granger's?'

'*Earning* is the word. We're run off our feet.'

'Shame you've got to be there tomorrow. You'd think they could have shut for Christmas Eve, at least. Haven't people bought all they want, by now?'

'Some people,' Simon said cynically, 'would start looking for a supermarket the moment they arrived on Venus in a space-rocket. There's no satisfying them. So naturally, where there's a demand, Granger's are going to be on hand to supply. We have our shareholders to keep sweet.'

Doris sniffed. 'How about keeping their branch managers sweet for once?'

He laughed. 'That's low on the agenda.'

'What I don't see is why you can't stop here overnight and drive in from here tomorrow morning. What's the point of going home?'

'If I stay here,' he explained, 'I shall get into a holiday mood and I shan't want to rise at the crack of dawn—which I must—to get to the store by eight. We're opening early, you see, so that we can close at four. Much better if I go straight from home. It also means the house will be occupied for another night.'

'I suppose that's not a bad idea. What time tomorrow will you be back here?'

'Easily by five.' Simon scrambled up. 'Seen the Christmas tree, Carol? In the lobby, as we came through? Let's go take a closer look.'

Left alone with Jo, Doris gave her daughter a further covert inspection. She was leaning back in a fatigued attitude, her eyes shut, her fingers loosening on the teacup and saucer which were starting to tilt dangerously. Stretching across, Doris rescued the china, causing Jo to reopen her eyes and give her a wan smile. 'Did I drift off? Must be the heat of the room. Where are the others?'

'Gone to admire the tree. Carol's thrilled, isn't she? Pretends not to be, but she still likes Christmas, you can see that.' Doris allowed a pause. 'Not sure I can say the same about you, though, love. Quite sure there's nothing wrong?'

'Mother, will you stop fussing? I'm fine.'

'You could have fooled me. Not surprising if you were having some kind of reaction, I reckon. All that upset, back in the summer . . .'

'I'd sooner not talk about it.'

'Enough to affect anybody.' Doris could be obstinate when she chose. 'These things, you know, they can catch up with you, later. Do you good to talk about it, if you ask me.'

'Mother, *please*.'

'You should have gone abroad afterwards, somewhere nice and warm, for a good long rest. All right, I'll shut up. I've said my say. That's what we're here for now, isn't it?—a rest. So we'll jolly well enjoy ourselves.'

In the darkness of the hotel bedroom, Jo listened to Carol's even breathing from the upper bunk in a corner.

Her stomach felt empty. The dinner to which they had sat down at seven had been well-chosen, delicately prepared, courteously served; and she had swallowed barely three mouthfuls. By pushing the food around, piling it here and there, she had done her best to disguise the full extent of her abstinence, but she was pretty sure it had not gone unnoticed by her mother. Although Doris had refrained from comment at the time, Jo had recognized the slight tightening of the mouth which foreshadowed an eventual resumption of the inquisition. She would have to be on her guard.

Meanwhile, there was the night to be got through. Another night; the latest in the interminable series. Lying there on her back, motionless on the unfamiliar springing, Jo broke out yet again into a sweat.

To get up would have been to disturb Carol. After a while, she knew from experience, her nightgown would dry on her. Cautiously putting out a hand, she located the small glass phial inside her handbag on the bedside table, uncapped it, shook out a capsule. Placing it on her tongue, she clamped her lips determinedly and embarked on a repeated swallowing action. Practice made it no easier. But finally the capsule slithered down her throat, catching on each side like a tumbling boulder, and she put her head back on the pillow.

She had a vision of Simon.

He was thrusting frozen turkeys into a metal skip. The skip stood in the middle of a field, and the earth surrounding it was in a state of upheaval, ploughed up by wheeled vehicles, heavy boots. Trying to run across the expanse, to reach the skip, Jo found herself bogged down, unable to move her legs except in agonizing slow-motion. Struggling, she moaned softly.

Tumbling out of the dream, she lay staring into the gloom. The time, she guessed, would be five-thirty or six. After taking a sleeping pill, she invariably came to at about this hour. Extricating her wrist from the sheets, she frowned at the illuminated digital face of her watch.

Eleven-forty.

Puzzled, she kept her gaze on the numerals. Presently they advanced to eleven-forty-one. Rolling back the bedclothes, Jo placed both feet cautiously on the floor, levered herself clear of the mattress, felt her head spin as the pill's effects backlashed on her. Having waited a few moments for an end to the gyrations, she began cautiously to dress. As she was zipping her skirt, the sound of a movement came from the bunk.

'Is it time to get up?'

'No, darling. Go back to sleep.'

'Why are you—'

'I have to go back downstairs. Just for a few minutes. I left something in the dining-room.'

'What?'

'I shan't be long.' Sliding her feet into her shoes, Jo felt for and picked up her handbag, groped her way across to the door. 'You won't be alone,' she whispered. 'I'll get Nan to come in while I'm gone. Sweet dreams.'

Closing the door firmly from outside, Jo walked along the dimly-lit corridor to the next door and gave it three raps. She had to repeat the action before a drowsy voice from within said, 'Who is it?'

'It's me—Jo.'

After a delay, the door latch rattled. A gap opened up, revealing part of a hair-mantled countenance screwed up in apprehension. 'What's the matter, love? Carol not well?'

'Carol's fine. Mother, could you do me a favour? Go next door and stay with her for a little while? You can sleep in my bed.'

'Sleep in your bed?' Perplexity ousted the alarm on Doris's features. 'Why? Where will you be?'

'I have to go out.'

'Out?'

'Back to the house. I think Simon might be in trouble.'

'What kind of trouble?' Her mother was peering at a travelling alarm clock in her left hand. 'Do you know it's nearly midnight?'

'I'm not sure what the problem is. I just have this feeling about him.'

Doris studied her narrowly. 'If you're that bothered, why not give him a ring?'

'I've tried, but there's no answer. I must go back and see.'

'Well, if you must . . . How will you get there, dear? There won't be any buses.'

'I'll manage. Can I rely on you, then, to stay with Carol? Here's the key to our room.' Jo thrust it into her mother's hand. 'Make yourself comfortable. I'll be there and back as quick as I can.'

'About what time—'

'Can't say. Depends what I find when I get there.'

'Do be careful. Shouldn't you try ringing the—'

'I'm off now. See you later.'

Heading for the first of the fire-doors, Jo avoided glancing back. After the third door, she remembered to turn left on to the staircase that took her after five flights into the reception area, spectral in the violet-shaded lamplight that was about to put up a weak struggle against the small hours of the morning. On the reception desk stood a small, brass bell. Shaking it, Jo created a tinkle which, after a minute or two, produced the night porter. He came from somewhere at the back, a frail-looking elderly man with thinning silver hair and the demeanour of a startled deer. He offered her a look of speechless inquiry.

'I'm terribly sorry,' she told him. 'I have to go out urgently—it's an emergency. Is it possible to get a cab?'

He scratched his ill-protected scalp. 'There's an all-night service on the Parade. They might send somebody. Staying here, are you?'

'Yes. Mrs Pettifer, Room 309. I've left my little girl up there, but her grandmother will be with her till I get back. Do you think you could phone the cab service for me?'

Approaching the desk, the night porter opened the register, scanned the entries briefly. 'Surely, Mrs Pettifer.' A touch of paternalism had entered his expression. 'Have a chair while I'm getting through. Mind you, they don't always answer. They say it's a 24-hour service but you know how it is, there are times when . . . Hang about. I'm getting the ringing tone. Now, the big question is . . .'

Jo barely heard him. Disregarding the available chairs, she wandered over to the Christmas tree in its tub, stood blindly inspecting it while wondering why she had lied to her mother about the phone call. Behind her, the night porter began talking more articulately. Presently he called across.

'Cabbie on his way, Mrs Pettifer. Five minutes.'

'Thank you.'

'At least, that's what they say. But I'd have that chair, if I was you. These days, there's no telling who you can count on.'

CHAPTER 22

Asking the cabbie to set her down at the gate, Jo got out shakily, bent down at his open window.

'Could you wait? I'm not sure how long I shall be.'

'Sure, I'll wait.'

'Shall I pay you now for the trip out?'

'Up to you, lady.' He was a youth of no more than twenty, a gaunt creature with a wandering nose and an insouciant manner. 'Here or when we get back—all the same to me. It's six quid,' he added helpfully, 'up to now.'

She paid him. 'Half an hour, I should think at the most.'

The Renault was not in the drive. Thanks to the wind which was ripping into her sheepskin jacket, the night was clear and starlit so that the outline of the house was visible, sketched against the dim mass of the Downs, Pausing before reaching the porch, she stood listening intently.

Above the gusts, a sound had reached her. Although unidentifiable, it had no place, she was convinced, in this locality at this hour. It recurred. Turning, she struck off to the right.

As she rounded the corner of the house, she stopped again with a gasp. The Renault was there, backed up against the extension site perimeter, its rear wheels resting on the single course of brick and breezeblock that had been laid on the foundation trenches. Now that her pupils had fully adjusted, she could make out details beyond the car. Chief among them was the upper half of a human figure. Near the rubble-strewn centre of the site, it was rising and falling in a series of jerky movements, to an accompaniment of the scraping noises that had seized her attention. For a few moments she stood motionless, looking on. Then she moved closer.

A piece of brick skidded noisily from under her heel. The half-figure on the site reared up before coming to rest as if skewered to the spot. She took another pace or two.

'Simon? It's only me.'

She saw him sag. 'For God's *sake*!'

'I was trying not to startle you. What are you doing?'

'You're meant to be asleep at the hotel.' Clambering out

of the pit, he moved towards her, grasping a shovel: one of the giant-bladed ones that Fenshaw's workforce had left around. 'Why the *hell* did you come back? Is Carol here?'

'No, I left her with Mother. I couldn't sleep, Simon. I had this weird feeling that you might be in some sort of . . .' Her voice tailed off. She stood gazing at him mutely, feeling the wind wrench at her hair.

'I never heard you coming.' Stepping over the brickwork, he joined her, stood resting his weight on the shovel. He was breathing heavily. She saw that he was clad in his gardening clothes: denim jacket, cords, gumboots. 'This lousy gale . . . How did you get here?'

'Minicab.'

'Did you pay him off?'

'I asked him to wait. I wasn't sure if . . .'

'*Christ!*'

'What is it?' The question emerged mechanically. She had started to shiver violently.

'Tonight, of all nights. You could have ruined everything. Where is he?'

'Down at the gate. He'll stay there. What are you up to, Simon? I thought you—'

'I'll tell you what I'm doing, you little idiot. I'm covering our tracks, for good and all. Putting the final touches to the whole arrangement. And you have to bring along an eye-witness . . .' The sentence ended in a choke. After a moment he resumed on a more controlled note. 'Is he parked outside the gate?'

'Yes. He's only a lad. I'm sure he won't want to budge till I get back. Simon, I can't—'

'All right, listen. Go back now, tell him you won't be needing him again. Then go inside the house and wait for me to finish. It shouldn't take much longer. I'm down several feet, into the chalk. Another half-hour—'

'You're burying her here, after all?'

'Good guess,' he said sarcastically. 'Top marks for deduction.'

'But what about Fenshaw?'

'What about him?'

'He or one of his men are bound to—'

'They won't find her. I'm going deep enough to be certain of that. Once she's in place—' Simon's gaze slid to the closed hatchback of the Renault—'I'll fill in again with soil and rubble, ram it down so it won't look as if it's been disturbed. Pretty soon they'll be concreting it over. Once that's done—'

'How can you talk about it like this?'

In the half-light, he peered at her. 'One of us has to talk about it. And think about it. And do something about it. Why don't you have faith in me?'

'I had faith in you, once,' she said bitterly.

He stood in silence, staring back at the pit. 'All that,' he said finally, 'is water under the bridge. What matters now is completing the job. Another hour and she'll be out of sight. A few more days and she'll be sealed under—permanently. That's all that need worry us.'

'What if they dig up the foundations again?'

'But they won't!' he exulted. 'That's the beauty of it.' He clutched her shoulders. 'You don't twig? Look at it from their standpoint. They've nursed their suspicions, they've been along, they've dug and they've excavated—they've literally taken the site apart. And what did they find? Nothing. They're not going to blunder through all that a second time, are they? Making jackasses of themselves once is bad enough.'

Limp in his grasp, Jo gazed past him at the earth and rubble mound beside the pit. Simon shook her.

'You still don't see, do you? The idea evolved. My original plan was a stopgap, that's all. Though it might have served, at a pinch. Then it came to me. Why not exploit the obvious?'

'The annexe was the very first place—'

'Of course it was. That's the whole point. It was so obvious, it bawled out to everyone. So I thought: If that's what they're all thinking, let 'em go on thinking—lead them on. Then, as soon as they—'

'What was the original plan?'

'To leave her where she was, naturally.'

'The septic tank?'

'Nearly as obvious,' Simon said disdainfully. 'I never gave it a second thought. You want to know where she's been, all these months? I'll tell you. She's been inside the extension.'

Jo's head jolted on her neck. 'But how could they have missed her when they—'

'Not this one, fathead. Fenshaw has done other work recently. Just about a year ago he enlarged the coldstore capacity at Granger's—remember? Quite an elaborate affair at the back, with access from the delivery yard.'

'But that's in constant—'

'As a good branch manager, I took an interest in the work, followed it through the various stages. Asked questions about it—quite innocently, at the time. I just wanted to be familiar with the layout. Which by the time they were through, I was.'

Jo looked at him speechlessly.

'Among other things,' Simon went on with an air of reminiscence, 'I watched them install a cavity floor. Insulation, you see. Fensaw explained it to me. Between the top of the coldstore and the base of the upper extension, which houses the staff accommodation, they left a four-foot space to allow for a kind of thermal blanket of air between one and the other, and also to house the various service pipes and so on. Not only that. For maintenance purposes, there's a means of access via a grating in the outside wall. Fenshaw reckoned it would never be needed. They had to include it under building by-laws, that's all. Get the picture?'

Her head shook involuntarily. Although she was absorbing the information, she couldn't yet come to terms with it. Simon misunderstood.

'It's a metal cover,' he said impatiently, 'opened by a special key. There are only two in existence, and I took charge of them both. Kept them at the back of a drawer in the office. Even Nigel Fielding doesn't know what became of them, and I doubt if anyone cares. Now do you see?'

Speech struggled on to Jo's lips. 'So when you drove away from here, that night . . .'

'I took the car straight to Granger's and round to the delivery yard. The place was deserted. I let myself in through the rear entrance, collected both the special keys from the office, then went back to the car and heaved her out. Once I'd opened the grating—'

'I don't want to hear any more.'

'—all I had to do was drag her inside and then find the most suitable spot. I chose the furthest corner, right behind a concrete pillar. After that I came out, relocked the grating, drove the car back to her flat . . . and that was it. I figured there was a better than evens chance that she wouldn't be discovered for years—if ever. By that time, I couldn't see how anyone could prove it was me who'd put her there.'

Jo sat heavily on a pile of bricks. 'What made you change your mind?'

'I didn't change it, exactly. I just got to thinking. As things stood, there was always going to be the slim possibility that maintenance work might be needed, and somebody would stumble on her. Whereas if I shifted her here, *after* the police had torn the place apart and retired in confusion . . . It was a far better scheme, and it only needed a bit of preparation to make it convincing—that was the beauty of it. A few deft touches, like hurrying on the project so as to draw general attention to it. And making use of the sky-gliders. I was rather pleased with that. It was only an outside chance, but I thought it was worth the effort. So I chose that evening when several of them were drifting around, and when one of them was right overhead I dragged that bundle across the lawn—you saw me, I believe, from the window—and went through the motions of planting it here, in one of the foundation trenches, so that . . .'

Simon broke off. 'You're not listening,' he said peevishly. 'I might as well save my breath. Why don't you go back to the gate, get rid of that cabbie? When you've done that—'

'Count me out, Simon.'

'I'll do it, then. You go inside. As soon as I'm through, I'll drive you back to the hotel, then come back here—'

'I don't mean that. I mean the thing itself. I can't allow it.'

Simon stood immobile. 'You're not going to *allow* it?' His voice was almost a whisper: but for its proximity to her right ear, it would have been lost in the wind. 'That's an odd thing to say. Who are you to dictate?'

'It's out of the question. How could we let Mother . . .' Jo sat moving her head from side to side. 'It's dreadful, Simon. I can't live with this.'

'There happens to be no alternative.'

'There is. We can come clean. Tell the authorities.'

'Are you out of your mind?'

'I shall be, if I have to exist under that kind of burden.'

Simon spoke slowly and distinctly. 'Two of us, remember, are involved in this. No, I'm wrong.' He lowered himself on to the bricks beside her. 'It's three. Have you stopped to consider the effect on Carol? Isn't she the one we're out to protect?'

'By landing her with a psychotic mother?'

'I'd be here to look after her.'

Jo steadied her head to look at him. 'You'd like that, wouldn't you? Carol all to yourself. No wife to inconveniently get in the way. Oh, you'd love that. I believe it's what you've been after, all along.'

'If you want to convince me you're crazy . . .'

'Everyone's off their head, aren't they, Simon? Everyone but you. You're the only one in step.'

'Mind what you're saying, Jo.'

'Do people always have to watch their tongues when they're talking to you?' Her utterances were getting wilder. She knew it, but couldn't stop herself. 'People like Polly? She stepped out of line, didn't she? The result for her was disastrous. Are you planning the same for me?'

'There's an old saying, Jo, you may have heard of.' Simon's voice was almost conversational; his hand was on her sleeve. 'When you've done it once, the second time is easy. You know, you'd only have yourself to blame.'

'Is that a threat?'

'Call it a warning.' His hand moved up her arm. 'Don't imagine I wouldn't do it.'

'Like you did to Polly?'

'Something like that.' His fingers had reached her throat. They were closing, tightening. 'There does come a time when people who are being obstructive have to be disposed of. Like branded goods. They have a shelf-life. When they start to deteriorate . . .'

Belatedly, Jo put up a fight. His right hand had moved in to support his left: together they were applying a squeeze, throttling the words she was trying to get out. 'You never . . . hit Polly . . . right? You strangled her in cold . . . in cold . . .'

'I'd no choice,' Simon said reasonably. 'Can't you see that? Can't anybody see?'

The scream began to erupt from her as the grip of his fingers slackened for an instant. At once they tightened again, killing the sound at birth. Struggling, she felt the bricks slide and collapse beneath her. Sprawled across their jutting corners, she had a moment in which to register the stab-pains in her flesh before her mind contracted to focus on the task of resisting the laryngeal pressure, staying alive. A noise of roaring gathered and swelled in her ears. Half a million people were cheering them on. But the stadium had become a cage. She had to get out.

The turnstile was blocked. It refused to budge. The roar of the crowd had penetrated to her very soul, ripping her apart. Where was the emergency exit? One should have been provided. If not, it was a scandal.

Lateral movement was impossible. She was wedged. This meant that each blow, as it fell on her, could not be avoided.

In one sense, there was less discomfort. The brick-corners were no longer pressing into her spine. Instead, she was lying on something relatively soft: it felt and smelt like newly-turned earth. The stench was all around her. It kept being renewed as, with metronomic remorselessness, the bombardment went on from above, adding still more weight to her thighs and stomach.

Her arms were immovable, locked against her hips. If she could free just one of them, hoist herself up . . .

Abruptly the situation worsened. The blows began to impact on her face. Gritty particles invaded her eyes; damp soil abused her nostrils. Her mouth, caught open without warning, filled with the stuff. Spitting it out, coughing and choking, she managed to turn her head aside, receiving the next onslaught on her ear.

Her nose was blocked. There was nowhere else to go.

A shake of the head achieved a small miracle. The blockage fell away, clearing her air passages. The next impact was due any second. It had to be now. Opening her mouth wide, she took in breath for a shriek.

CHAPTER 23

A detailed account of the trial was carried in the *Beacon*. Particular emphasis was given to the role of Nick Denton (22), minicab driver, of Seaview Gardens, Southweald East.

His suspicions were alerted, Mr Denton told the court, when he identified the address to which he had driven Mrs Pettifer as the one that had figured recently in a highly-publicized police operation to solve the mystery of Miss Gathercole's disappearance.

'I knew the background to the case,' said Mr Denton, 'because of what I'd read about the cops digging around under the extension, back in the summer. It interested me, and I kept cuttings about it.'

When Mrs Pettifer asked him to wait at the gate while she walked up to the house, he began to feel that something questionable might be going on.

'I'd spotted the nameplate on the gatepost in my headlamps—that kind of brought it all back to me. I started asking myself what Mrs Pettifer was up to, getting herself taken back there from a hotel in town at dead of night.

'She'd no luggage, except for a handbag. And she looked funny to me—a bit wild-eyed and staring, like, as if she'd had some kind of a shock.'

Mr Denton said he waited inside his cab for about ten minutes before deciding to go and investigate. 'I didn't fancy sticking around there for an hour or more, on the offchance she'd want me to take her back. So I walked through the gate and I was just starting up the drive to look for her when I heard this scream.'

Following the direction of the cry, Mr Denton ran to the side of the house where the annexe was being built. Although it was fairly dark, he was able to see the figure of a man at the centre of the site, shovelling earth 'like the clappers' into a hole.

'I shouted out to him and he looked round. He never said a word. He just kind of leapt towards me, swinging the shovel like it was a bicycle-chain or something. I just had time to duck, and the shovel flew over my head and hit a concrete-mixer behind me.

'Then I managed to get in close and sort of grappled

with him. He was fighting mad, so I had my work cut out.'

Mr Denton, a squash fanatic who works out twice weekly at a local keep-fit centre, told the court he got Pettifer in a half-nelson and was dragging him towards the house when the defendant broke free and darted away across the garden. On the point of giving chase, the witness paused when he heard another call from the hole on the site, and went to investigate.

'I was just able to see the side of this woman's face and a bit of her hair. The rest of her was covered in about a foot of earth. She had it in her eyes and mouth—she was trying to spit it away when I got to her.

'I had to dig the earth away before I could drag her clear. She couldn't say much. I think her throat was all swollen. She did tell me, "She's in there. He put me on top of her." I wasn't sure what she meant, but I could make a guess.'

As he left the witness stand, Mr Denton was complimented on his actions by the Judge.

The court heard from Detective Chief Inspector Walter Dean that for a time after his arrest Pettifer was assessed as being in need of psychiatric treatment. By the time he was brought to trial, however, he had shown marked signs of improvement in this respect, and had cooperated fully with the police.

He had absolved his wife of any responsibility for the killing of Miss Gathercole or its aftermath. 'Jo knew about it,' he was said to have told the chief inspector, 'but that was all. She kept quiet for my sake and Carol's, but in the end it got too much for her. She just couldn't take it, and I lost my head.'

Despite the decomposition of the body, Chief Inspector Dean told the court, forensic examination had been able to prove that Miss Gathercole had in fact been strangled, not killed accidentally as she fell, as Pettifer had at first claimed. Faced with this evidence, the defendant had made a full admission of guilt, in which he said: 'I should like to make it clear that it was never my intention to bury my wife alive. I thought I had strangled her before I put her in the hole. When she screamed, I just panicked. I know it makes no difference, but I should like her to be aware of that.'

Sentencing Pettifer to life imprisonment for murder and attempted murder, the Judge told him: 'You are a man who was cold-bloodedly out for all he could get, at the expense of others. Apart from your vaunted affection for your daughter, which you have tried to present as motivation for your actions, I can find no mitigating factor in your conduct.'

Pettifer showed no emotion as he left the dock.

'Two years' probation,' said Doris, in the taxi on the way to the station. 'Might have been a lot worse.'

Jo continued to gaze ahead. Doris tried again.

'Quite fair, I reckon he was, that judge. I mean, he could obviously see the strain you were under at the time, what with trying to keep the family together, not knowing what to do for the best . . .'

'What time is our train?'

Doris blinked. 'Three-twenty,' she said, recovering fast. 'Looking forward to Guildford, are you, love? Make you a nice cup of tea when we get home.'

'How long does it take?'

'What, the journey? About an hour. We'll be there in time to give Carol a welcome when Mrs Pearson brings her back. Lucky she was around. She's a nice soul, and Carol gets on well with her daughter, even though she's a bit older. Mrs Pearson was telling me—'

'Are those Pressmen still following us?'

Doris turned to look. 'Can't be certain. Don't fret, love. If anyone accosts us at the station, they'll get the rough end of my tongue. You've got your mum to look after you, now.'

Jo rested her forehead on her mother's shoulder, and wept.